MW01286514

MASTERED BY HER MATES

INTERSTELLAR BRIDES® PROGRAM: BOOK 6

GRACE GOODWIN

Mastered by Her Mates
Copyright © 2017 by Grace Goodwin

This book was written by a human and not Artificial Intelligence (A.I.).

This book may not be used to train Artificial Intelligence (A.I.).

Interstellar Brides® is a registered trademark
of KSA Publishing Consultants Inc.
All Rights Reserved. No part of this book may be reproduced or transmitted in
any form or by any means, electrical, digital or mechanical including but not
limited to photocopying, recording, scanning or by any type of data storage and
retrieval system without express, written permission from the author.

Published by KSA Publishers
Goodwin, Grace
Mastered by Her Mates
Cover design copyright © 2020 by Grace Goodwin
Images/Photo Credit: Deposit Photos: faestock, sdecoret

Publisher's Note:
This book was written for an adult audience. The book may contain explicit
sexual content. Sexual activities included in this book are strictly fantasies
intended for adults and any activities or risks taken by fictional characters
within the story are neither endorsed nor encouraged by the author or
publisher.

SUBSCRIBE TODAY!

P PATREON

*H*i there! Grace Goodwin here. I am SO excited to invite you into my intense, crazy, sexy, romantic, imagination and the worlds born as a result. From Battlegroup Karter to The Colony and on behalf of the entire Coalition Fleet of Planets, I welcome you! Visit my Patreon page for additional bonus content, sneak peaks, and insider information on upcoming books as well as the opportunity to receive NEW RELEASE BOOKS before anyone else! See you there! ~ Grace

Grace's PATREON: https://www.patreon.com/gracegoodwin

GET A FREE BOOK!

JOIN MY MAILING LIST TO STAY INFORMED OF NEW RELEASES, FREE BOOKS, SPECIAL PRICES AND OTHER AUTHOR GIVEAWAYS.

http://freescifiromance.com

FIND YOUR INTERSTELLAR MATCH!

YOUR mate is out there. Take the test today and discover your perfect match. Are you ready for a sexy alien mate (or two)?

VOLUNTEER NOW!
interstellarbridesprogram.com

1

manda Bryant, Interstellar Bride Processing Center, Earth

THIS COULDN'T BE REAL. But it *felt* real. The warm air on my sweaty skin. The redolent scent of fucking. The soft sheets beneath my knees. The hard body at my back. I was blind-folded, the silk making everything as black as night. But I didn't need sight to know a cock was buried deep in my pussy. A big, thick cock.

It was real. *It was real!*

I was kneeling on a bed, the man behind me, fucking me. His hips shifted, rocking his cock over every delicious nerve ending, my inner walls rippling around him. His hard thighs were beneath me, an arm wrapped about my waist and cupping my breast, anchoring me in place so I couldn't move. I could only take it as he bottomed out deep inside me. I could go nowhere—not that I wished to. Why would I want to leave? It felt *so* good. *His cock* felt so good stretching me open, fill-ing me.

It wasn't just the man behind me making me lose my mind. A second man—yes, I was with two men!—kissed his way down my belly. Hot licks of his tongue in my navel, then lower and lower...

How long could he take for his lips to finish their journey to my clit?

That little nub pulsed and throbbed in eagerness. Hurry, tongue, hurry!

How could this be real? How could two men be touching me, licking me, fucking me? They were. Because the man at my back wrapped his strong hands around my inner thighs and opened me even wider for the other to explore me with his hands and tongue...and found my clit.

Finally! I rocked my hips forward, wanting more.

"Hold still, mate. We know you want to come, but you will wait." The deep voice at my ear breathed the heated words against the side of my neck, even as he shifted his hips, spreading me open with his giant cock.

Wait? I couldn't wait! Every time the cock plunged deep, the tongue on my clit flicked, then licked. No woman could survive a cock plus a flick and lick.

I moaned. Whimpered, tried to circle my hips into the pleasure. I loved it. I wanted them both inside me. Was desperate for them to claim me, to make me theirs forever.

For a split second my mind rebelled, as I had no mates. I hadn't taken a lover in over a year. I'd never taken two men at once. Never considered wanting both of my holes filled. Who were these men? Why was I—

The tongue was gone from my clit and I cried out. "No!"

Soon, that mouth was on my nipple, and I felt the man before me smile against my tender skin. He tugged and suckled me until I whimpered, begging for more. I rode the razor's edge, my body on the brink of orgasm. The cock filling me was incredible, but it wasn't enough.

I needed.

"More."

The plea left my lips before I could regain control and a dark part of me thrilled at the punishment I knew the demand would bring. How did I know that? I was so confused, but didn't want to take any time to think, just enjoy.

Immediately, a strong hand wrapped in my hair, tugging my head back with a painful sting as the man behind me twisted my head to his, teasing my lips with his own.

"You do not make demands, mate. You submit." He kissed me, his tongue a hard, dominant intrusion in my mouth. He thrust as he fucked me, his tongue and his cock invading my body as one before withdrawing to the edge and plunging within once more.

My other mate—wait, mate?—used his fingers to spread my pussy lips even wider. He licked my clit, then blew on it gently as the cock fucking me slammed deep, then pulled nearly free. Lick. Blow. Lick. Blow. I was near tears, my arousal too intense to be contained.

"Please, please. *Please.*"

A single tear fell and escaped the edges of my blindfold, wetting the skin where my cheek and my mate's touched. He broke the kiss instantly, his warm tongue tracing the path with a loud rumble. "Ah begging. We love our mate to beg. That means you are ready."

The one I imagined must be on his knees before me, the one torturing me with his mouth, spoke to me then.

"Do you accept my claim, mate? Do you give yourself to me and my second freely, or do you wish to choose another primary male?"

"I accept your claim, warriors." My vow spoken, my mates growled, their control pushed to its limit.

"Then we claim you in the rite of naming. You belong to us and we shall kill any other warrior who dares to touch you."

"May the gods witness and protect you." The chorus of voices sounded around us and I gasped as the man on his knees before me nipped at my inner thighs with his teeth in a dark promise of more pleasure.

"Come for us now, mate. Show them all how your mates bring you pleasure." The mate at my back issued the order just before his mouth crushed my lips in a searing kiss.

Wait, what others?—Before I could finish the thought the other man's mouth clamped down, hard on my clit, sucking and flicking his tongue, pushing me over the edge.

I screamed, but the sound was lost to me as waves of ecstasy crashed through me. My body became taut like a bow, only my pussy walls rippled and clenched the cock that continued to fuck me. Hard, so hard and yet the tongue that continued to flick my clit was so soft and gentle.

Heat bloomed on my skin, bright white flickered behind my eyelids, my fingers tingled. Hell, my entire body tingled. But my mates weren't finished with me, they did not allow me to catch my breath before I was lifted off the large cock and turned around. I heard the rustle of sheets, felt the bed shift, then I was lifted on top of him. With hands on my hips, I was lowered back onto his cock. In seconds, he had filled me again, pumping up into me as my other mate reached around between us and fingered my clit. I was so primed, so sensitive, that I was instantly on edge.

Desire spiraled within, and I tensed, holding my breath as fire rushed through me. I was going to come again. They worked me so simply, yet they knew my body, knew how to touch me, how to lick and suck me. How to fuck me so perfectly that all I could do was come. Again and again. "Yes. Yes. Yes!"

"No."

The command was like a leash and my orgasm came to heel, waiting. A firm hand spanked my bare bottom. The sound of it was a loud crack, the feel of it a bright flash of pain. Three times. Four. When he stopped, the prickly heat of it spread through me. I *should* have hated it. He'd spanked me! But no. My traitorous body *liked* it, for the extra sensation went straight to my breasts, my clit. My whole body felt like it was on fire and I wanted more. I wanted their commands. I wanted their control. I wanted it all. I *needed* both of my mates to fill me, to fuck me, to claim me. I wanted to be theirs forever.

Firm hands locked onto my ass, pulling my cheeks open for the mate behind me. Even as the one lying beneath me held me open, he ground his pelvis, fucking me with small strokes into a blissful euphoria. My pussy was stuffed so full, how could my other mate fit in my ass? How could the two of them claim me properly without causing me pain? Somehow I knew that I would like it. Memories of a large plug filling me, spreading me open, getting me ready for this, reassured me. I'd liked the plug filling me as they fucked me, so I would surely die of pleasure when I had two cocks in me.

The need wasn't just to fuck both of my mates at once. It was to stake my claim and make these men mine forever. Only their double penetration would do it. I *loved* these men. I wanted them. I wanted them both.

My mate's finger explored my tight ass, a virgin to a cock, but I knew he would fit. Both men were powerful and dominant, and yet gentle. The mating oil he used to work one finger inside, then another, was a welcome heat in my body. I panted as the warmth of his fingers slowly spread me open, ensuring I was truly ready to be claimed.

Arms wrapped around my back and the mate beneath me pulled me down so I rested on his broad chest. His hand stroked up and down the length of my spine.

"Arch your back. Yes, like that." The fingers slipped from my ass and while I felt open and ready, I felt empty. I *needed* more. The mate behind me continued. "When I get my cock into this snug little ass, you will be ours forever. You are the link, connecting us as one."

The blunt head of his cock pressed forward, slowly, filling me until I thought I would die from pleasure. The pre-cum on the tip of his cock slipped inside me and made fire spread through my nerve endings, like a jolt of electricity that went straight to my clit.

I tried to hold on, I tried to behave, to deny the pleasure spiraling through me, to wait for permission, but I could not.

I came with a scream, my pussy convulsing so hard I nearly forced the second cock from my body with the force of the muscle spasms. I couldn't think, couldn't breathe, and each thrust of my mates' cocks pushed me higher, until I came again—

"Yes!"

"Miss Bryant."

The woman's voice seemed to appear out of thin air, filling my mind with the cold chill of reality. I ignored it, reaching for the ecstasy I'd just experienced, but the more I tried to focus on my mates, the harder it became to feel them. Their scent was gone. Their heat, gone. Their cocks, gone. I cried out a denial as hard, cold fingers wrapped around my shoulder, shaking me.

"Miss Bryant!"

No one touched me like that. No one.

Years of martial arts training kicked in and I tried to swing my arm to block the assault on my shoulder. I did not want those cold hands touching me. I didn't want anyone touching me, anyone but my mates. Those strong hands that were so gentle.

The sharp pain of restraints cutting into my wrists brought me back to reality. I couldn't knock the hand away, I couldn't punch her. I was trapped. Restrained. Cuffed to some kind of chair. Defenseless.

Blinking, I looked around, trying to regain my bearings.

God, my pussy was pulsing with desire and my breathing was ragged. I was naked beneath some type of hospital gown, cuffed to an exam table that looked more like a dentist's chair than a hospital bed. Air whooshed in and out of my lungs in rapid panting sounds as I tried to calm my racing heart. My engorged clit throbbed. I wanted to touch it with my fingers, to finish what the men had started, but that was impossible. In the restraints, all I could do was grip my hands into fists.

I'd had an orgasm, right here in this damn chair, pinned and naked like a freak. I was a five-year intelligence operative. I'd been assigned this mission because my country was trusting me to maintain control, to do what needed to be done out there in space. Not fall apart and beg for orgasms from the first alien whose hard cock made me so hot I forgot my own name.

I recognized the signs and knew my face was turning a dark shade of pink at the thought of not just *one* dominant, commanding alpha male making my pussy weep, making me beg. One lover? A hint of normalcy? No. Not me. I had to make things interesting and imagine fucking two of them at the same time. God, my mother would be rolling over in her grave right now.

"Miss Bryant?" There was that voice again.

"Yes." Resigned, I turned my head to find a group of seven women watching me with obvious curiosity. They all wore dark gray uniforms with a strange burgundy insignia over their left breasts. I'd seen that symbol often enough the last two months, it was the mark of the Interstellar Coalition, indicating they were all employees of the Interstellar Bride Program's testing center, Wardens, they were called, as if signing with the Coalition were a jail sentence. The women were a cross-section of races, black, white, Asian, Hispanic. They represented all the races of Earth. How fucking perfect. A pale-skinned woman with dark brown hair and sympathetic gray eyes was the one speaking to me. I knew her name, but she didn't know that. I knew a lot of things I wasn't supposed to know.

I licked my lips, swallowed. "I'm awake."

My voice was scratchy as if I'd been crying out. Oh God. Had I really screamed when I came? Had I begged and moaned as these stoic women bore witness?

"Excellent." The Warden looked like she was in her late twenties, perhaps a year or two younger than me. "I am Warden Egara, and I am in charge of the Interstellar Bride Program here on Earth. The processing program indicates a successful match has been made for you, but since you are the first volunteer bride that's been matched using the Interstellar Bride protocols, we will need to ask you a few additional questions."

"Okay." I took a deep breath, let it out. The desire was slowly seeping away, the sweat on my skin gone. Goose bumps rose on my flesh in the cool, air-conditioned room that worked so hard to stave off the heat of Miami in August. The hard chair felt sticky and the gown scratchy against my sensitive skin. Leaning my head back, I waited.

According to the aliens promising to "protect" the Earth from an alleged threat known as the Hive, these human women who stood before me had been mated to alien warriors in the past, and were now widows who had volunteered to serve the Coalition here on Earth.

Oh, and there were more than two-hundred and sixty alien races fighting in the Coalition forces, but they claimed only a fraction were compatible for mating with humans. That seemed odd. And how did they know, if a human had never been sent to space before?

The Coalition ships had shown up a couple months ago, on a Wednesday, June 4 at 6:53 p.m. Eastern Time. Yes, I remember the time exactly, like I'd forget the moment when I found out there really were others "out there". I'd been hitting the treadmill at the gym, twenty-three minutes into my ninety-minute workout when the television screens lining the walls had all gone crazy. Every channel was suddenly alien ships, alien landings all over the world, and fucking huge, seven-foot tall, yellow alien warriors in black camo armor walking off their little shuttles like they owned us already.

Whatever. They spoke our languages and claimed to have just won a battle in our solar system. Once they had a television crew in their face, they demanded a meeting with every major world leader. A few days later, at that meeting in Paris, the aliens had refused to acknowledge the sovereignty of any country and demanded Earth choose one supreme leader, a Prime, they called it. One representative for the entire world. Countries were irrelevant. Our laws? Irrelevant. We were part of their Coalition now, and must follow their laws.

That meeting had been broadcast live all over the world in every major language, not by our television stations on Earth, but by their control of our satellite network. Angry and terrified world leaders broadcast live on international television in every country?

Let's just say, the meeting had not gone well.

My blood boiled as I watched. Riots erupted. People were scared. The President had called out the National Guard and every police force and fire department in the country had been working overtime for two weeks. That was about how long it took people to realize the aliens weren't going to just blow us up and take what they wanted.

But then...this. Brides. Soldiers. They said they didn't want our planet, claimed to be protecting us, but they wanted our soldiers to fight in their war and human women mated to their warriors. And I was the crazy bitch who'd volunteered to be the first human sacrifice.

Giant, yellow alien sex? Because that's what brides did, have sex with their mate. Yeah, it wasn't a *husband* but a *mate*. Coming right up.

Yay, me.

The sarcastic thought made me shiver and I shook my head to clear it. I was on a mission, a critical assignment. The thought of fucking one of those huge warriors with a massive chest, golden skin and dominant expression should not excite me. I didn't know who I'd get, but from all of the TV footage, they were *all* big. They were *all* dominant.

But it did excite me and I hoped that I'd find at least some pleasure in this mission. If I didn't, I would endure. But if I could ride one of their huge cocks to a mind-numbing orgasm once in a while, would that be so bad? I'd consider it a perk of the job. I was giving up my life, my home, my whole fucking planet for the next few years. A couple of decent orgasms shouldn't be too much to ask. Right?

I'd spent years serving my country, and I was confident in my ability to handle any situation, adapt to anything. I was a survivor, and more, I wasn't buying their story, and neither had my superiors at the agency. Where was the proof? Where were these horrible Hive creatures?

The Coalition commanders showed videos to our leaders that any junior high kid with the right software could have created. No one on Earth had ever seen a Hive soldier in the flesh, and the Coalition commanders refused to give us the weapons and technology we would need to defend ourselves from such a deadly threat.

Me? I'd always been a skeptic, and extremely pragmatic. If something needed to be done to protect my country, I did it. I'd been worried about the usual, terrorism, global warming, illegal arms dealers, drug smuggling, international hacker taking control of our energy or banking systems. And now? Aliens. I still couldn't quite wrap my head around that, despite the fact that I'd watched hours of videos and interviews with their huge, golden commanders from a planet called Prillon Prime. Seven foot of sexy on a stick.

So...one. I'd seen *one* race of aliens, out of the supposed hundreds. Even their processing center people, these Wardens, were humans they'd most likely brainwashed.

For a first contact scenario, the Prillon warriors weren't doing much convincing. One would think they would have a better propaganda strategy going. Either that, or they didn't give a shit what we thought because they were actually telling the truth and a very aggressive, nasty race of aliens along the lines of the Borg from *Star Trek* was waiting in the wings to destroy all life on Earth.

I was going with theory number one, but we couldn't eliminate the possibility of theory number two. Earth did not want to be *assimilated.*

My job? To find out the truth. And the only way anyone was going to do that was actually to go out into space. They weren't taking soldiers yet, so lucky me, I was going the other route. The Interstellar Bride Program.

This was not how I'd envisioned my big day. No, I'd wanted the usual, a ridiculously expensive white dress, flowers, corny music played on harps and a bunch of family members in the pews I was paying a fortune to feed but that I hadn't seen in a decade.

Speaking of weddings, how the hell had the women standing before me supposedly been mated to aliens, when, until a couple of months ago, humanity hadn't even known that aliens existed?

"How do you feel?" Warden Egara asked, and I realized I'd probably been staring off into space for a few minutes as my thoughts chased each other in circles inside my head.

"Feel?" I repeated.

Really? I took a moment to take stock of my body. My pussy was dripping wet and the gown scrunched up beneath me was soaked. My clit throbbed in time with my pulse, and I'd just had two of the most incredible orgasms of my life. Good day to be a spy.

"As you're well aware, you are the first human woman to volunteer for the Interstellar Bride Program, so we're curious as to how you experienced the processing."

"I'm your guinea pig?"

They all smiled, but it seemed only Warden Egara had been elected to speak. "In a sense, yes. Please tell us how you feel after your testing."

"I feel fine."

My gaze raked over their earnest expressions, but the one woman, the one with the dark hair who'd woken me from the dream, Warden Egara, cleared her throat.

"During the, um, simulation—"

Ah, so that's what they were calling it.

"—did you experience the dream as a third-party witness? Or did it feel like you were really, you know, there?"

I sighed. What else could I do? I *felt* like I'd just had mind-blowing monkey sex with two huge alien warriors...and I'd loved it. "I was there. It was all happening to me."

"So, you felt like you were the bride? That your mate was claiming you?"

Claiming? That was *way* more than just claiming. That was...wow.

"Mates. And yes." Crap. Heat ran up my neck to pink my cheeks again. Mates? As in two. Now, why had I admitted to that?

Warden Egara's shoulders relaxed. "Two mates? Correct?"

"That's what I said."

She clapped her hands together and I turned to see a look of happy relief on her face. "Excellent! You were matched to Prillon Prime, so everything appears to be working perfectly."

Big golden warrior for me, just like the ones on TV? Check.

And how convenient that I wasn't matched to one of the *other* races. I truly had to wonder if the others even existed.

The Warden turned to one of the other women. "Warden Gomez, will you please inform the Coalition that the protocol has been integrated into the human population and appears to be fully functional. We should be able to process volunteer brides at all seven centers within a few weeks."

"Of course, Warden Egara. It will be my pleasure," Warden Gomez replied, her response thick with a Portuguese accent. "I am eager to return to Rio, to see my family."

Warden Egara sighed happily and walked away from me to lift a tablet monitor from the table on the edge of the room before returning to me. "All right. Since you're the first woman in the Interstellar Bride Program, I hope you'll be patient as we work through the protocols."

She smiled, and the look on her face was radiant, as if she were thrilled to be sending me off planet to be married to an alien I'd never met. Had all these women *really* been married to aliens? Why were they the ones asking questions? I wanted to know more. Up until a couple months ago, aliens were only little green men in movies, or disgusting things with tentacles that either hunted us, or deposited larvae that made our chest explode.

Ugh. I watched too many sci-fi movies. And now that I was totally creeped out, I decided now was a good time to stall. "Um... I need to talk to my father before we go any further. He will be worried."

"Oh, of course!" She stepped back and lowered the tablet, holding it at her side. "You should say your goodbyes, Amanda. Once we begin the protocol, you'll be processed and trans-ported immediately."

"Today? Now?" Oh crap. I wasn't ready for *now*.

She nodded. "Yes. Now. I'll go get your family." She left me alone, the other women streaming out in a line behind her. I stared at the ceiling, clenching and unclenching my fists, trying to remain calm.

My father? Yeah, so not true. He wasn't my family, but the Warden didn't know that. I hadn't been home to New York in two months. Home? It was more of an apartment where I slept when I was not on assignment. Which was...practically never. But hey, at least I wouldn't miss it.

My boss had called me in during my only three days off in the last three months, flown me straight from New York to the Pentagon for two months of intense debriefing and preparation. When I'd landed in Miami, they'd picked me up in a limousine. I should have known I'd wouldn't go home again before the processing occurred. Hell, I *had* known, but some poor little corner of my heart had still been hoping this was all some big fucking joke.

No such luck, and there wasn't anything I could do about it. It wasn't like you could tell the Company no. My job wasn't the kind where you could just quit. It wasn't the Mafia, but a spy didn't just resign and become a school teacher either. There was *always* a new assignment. A job. A new threat, a new enemy.

But sending me out into space as an alien bride? That was off the charts, even for them. Still, I knew why I'd been chosen. I spoke five languages fluently, had been an active field agent for five years, and more importantly, I was single, with no family ties and nothing to lose. My parents were dead and I was a woman. Seemed the aliens only requested female brides, and I wondered if any of them were gay? Did the gay warriors request brides? Or did they just hook up with their fellow warriors and call it good?

So many questions without answers. That's why they needed me.

Guinea pig? Sacrificial lamb? Yep. That about summed it up.

The heavy door swung open and my boss walked in, followed by a man I recognized, but barely knew. They both wore plain blue suits, white button-down shirts, one yellow and one paisley tie. Their hair was graying at the temples, both styles military short. They were unremarkable, men you'd walk past on a busy sidewalk and never take note of, unless you looked in their eyes. They were two of the most dangerous men I knew, and I knew quite a few in my line of work. They'd been chosen by the President to do whatever needed to be done to ascertain the truth about this new alien threat.

Apparently I wasn't the only one who wasn't buying the— *we're here to save you, just give us your soldiers and your women*— line of bullshit these aliens were spewing. Not one government on Earth was happy and the U.S. and her allies were determined to discover the truth. And, with my mixed heritage of an Irish father and half black, half Asian mother, they'd all agreed I represented a whole lot of humanity. They'd requested I volunteer for this assignment.

Lucky me.

"Amanda."

"Robert." I nodded at the silent man to his right and had no idea if I even knew his real name. "Allen."

Robert cleared his throat. "How did the processing go?"

"Fine. Warden Egara says I've been matched to Prillon Prime."

Allen nodded. "Excellent. The Prillon warriors are in command of the entire Coalition Fleet. We were also informed that they keep their brides with them on their battleships, on the front lines of this alleged war. You should have access to weapons, tactical information and their most advanced technologies."

Great. Two months ago, when I had agreed to take this mission, I would have been thrilled. But now? My heart beat a little too fast at the idea that what I really *wanted* was unlimited access to two smoking-hot, dominant alien warriors' bodies...

Robert crossed his arms over his chest and glared down at me, trying to put on his protective father-figure face. I'd seen through that act years ago, but I played along as he continued. "While the Bride Program appears to be up and running, they are not yet ready to begin processing our soldiers for their military. They won't complete testing over there for a few more days. Once they do, we'll send two of our men along to infiltrate the unit and assist with your mission. The men have already been selected. They're good men, Amanda. Completely black."

"Understood." And I did. Black, as in special operations assets so critical to national security that they didn't officially exist. They were sending super soldiers to cover all their bases. Me in the enemy's bed, the soldiers in their military units.

"One way or another, find out the true extent of the Hive threat to Earth, send back weapons and engineering schematics from their ships, and anything else you can get your hands on." I knew my orders, but Robert didn't hesitate to repeat them one last time.

The aliens had magnanimously offered Earth protection from the Hive, but repeatedly refused to share their advanced weaponry or transporter technology with Earth. Earth's governments were not pleased. Nothing like being on top of the world, a superpower for decades, then being sent with your tail between your legs to the back of the bus. There wasn't just *us* anymore, humans. It was an entire universe of planets and races and cultures and...enemies.

Robert lifted his arm to squeeze my shoulder. "We're counting on you. The whole world is counting on you."

"I know, sir." No pressure, right? "I won't let you down."

Warden Egara chose that moment to return, her bright smile and cheery demeanor brittle and a little too shiny. I wasn't sure what she thought of my two visitors, but whatever it was, she wasn't pleased.

"So, are you ready, Miss Bryant?"

"Yes."

"If you'll excuse us, gentlemen?" When the two suits were gone she turned to me, the tablet in her lap and her smile genuine. "You okay? I know it can be tough leaving your family."

She looked over her shoulder at the closed door, and I realized she was referring to Robert, my supposed father.

"Oh, um...yeah. I'm fine. We're not that...close."

The warden studied me intently for a moment, must have seen I had no emotional ties, and continued. "Okay. So, to begin the protocol—for the record, state your name, please."

"Amanda Bryant."

"Miss Bryant, are you now, or have you ever been married?"

"No." Engaged once, but that had ended the night I told my fiancé what I did for a living. I wasn't supposed to tell him I was a spy, so bad on me...

"Do you have any biological offspring?"

"No."

She tapped her screen a few times without looking at me. "I am required to inform you, Miss Bryant, that you will have thirty days to accept or reject the mate chosen for you by the Interstellar Bride Program's matching protocols."

"Okay. And what if I reject the match? What happens? Will I be sent back to Earth?"

"Oh no. There will be no return to Earth. As of this moment, you are no longer a citizen of Earth."

"Wait. What?" I did not like the sound of that. Never come back? Ever? I'd figured a year or two in the field and I'd come home, retire on a sandy beach and sip piña coladas for a few years. Now I couldn't come home? My citizenship revoked? Could they even *do* that?

Suddenly I was shaking, and not with excitement or arousal, with dread. No one at the office said I wouldn't be coming back. They had to have known. God, after five years of service, they were just sending me to outer space as what... some kind of noble sacrifice? Those assholes at the agency had conveniently forgotten to mention this one, small detail.

"You, Miss Bryant, are now a warrior bride of Prillon Prime, subject to that planet's laws, customs and protections. If your mate is unacceptable, you may request a new primary mate after thirty days. You may continue the mating process, on Prillon Prime, until you find a mate who *is* acceptable."

I tugged at the restraints on the table, my mind racing a thousand miles an hour. Could I escape? Could I change my mind? Forever? Never come home? The reality of leaving Earth behind forever pressed in on my chest until I couldn't get enough air. The room started spinning.

"Miss Bryant— Oh, dear." Warden Egara's hand flew over her tablet for a few seconds before she put it down on the table behind her. "You'll be fine, love. I promise."

Promise? She'd promise that I was going to be fine with being transported into outer space and never...ever coming home?

The wall behind me lit with a strange blue light and the chair beneath me jolted a bit as it began to move sideways, toward the light.

I couldn't look. Instead, I closed my eyes and focused on filling my lungs with fresh air. I didn't panic. Ever. This was so unlike me.

But then, I'd never had multiple orgasms in a damn testing chair either. And I'd never, ever fantasized about taking two lovers at once. The way they'd made me feel had been like nothing I'd ever felt on Earth. Would it be like that? Would my men make me feel that way?

The warden's warm fingers wrapped around my wrist

gently and I opened my eyes to find her concerned face hovering nearby. She smiled at me, like a preschool teacher smiling at a scared four-year-old on the first day of class.

"Don't worry so much. The match was ninety-five percent. Your mate will be perfect for you, and you for him. The system works. When you wake up, you'll be with your mate. He will take care of you. You're going to be happy, Amanda. I promise."

"But—"

"When you wake, Amanda Bryant, your body will have been prepared for Prillon Prime's matching customs and your mate's requirements. He will be waiting for you." Her voice had become more formal, as if she recited another protocol by rote.

"Wait—I," My voice stalled as a large metallic arm with a gigantic needle on the end appeared to be headed for the side of my face. "What is that?" I knew I sounded panicked, couldn't help it. I did not do needles.

"Don't worry, dear, I am inserting a Neuroprocessing Unit that will integrate with the language centers of your brain, allowing you to speak and understand any language. We call it an NPU."

Okay. Holy shit, I guess I was about to be implanted with some of their advanced technology. I held completely still as the needle pierced the side of my head, just behind and below my ear.

If all else failed, I could come home and Robert could cut the damn chips, or whatever they were, out of my head. Sad thing was, I knew he'd do it.

But what if I never came back? What if the aliens were telling the truth? What if I fell in love with my mate...?

My chair slipped inside a small enclosure and I was lowered, chair and all, into a warm, soothing tub of strange blue water. "Your processing will being in three...two...one."

ommander Grigg Zakar, Coalition Fleet, Sector 17

THE HIVE scout ship blazed by, just off my fighter's right wingtip and I let him go, much more concerned with the larger, more heavily armored attack cruiser before me.

"Hive command ship in range. I'm going in." I informed my command crew back on board the *Battleship Zakar*, my battleship, so they could coordinate the rest of the battle wings around my attack.

"Don't do anything stupid this time." The dry tone in my ear belonged to my best friend, and top-ranked doctor in this sector of space, Conrav Zakar. Rav, he'd always been Rav to me, was also my cousin. We'd been fighting together for more than ten years, and been friends longer.

I couldn't help that the corner of my mouth tipped up into a wry smile. Even in the midst of battle, that asshole could amuse me.

"If I do, just be ready to patch me up."

"One of these days, I'll let you bleed out." He chuckled and my smile spread to a grin behind the clear mask of my pilot's helmet.

"No, you won't." I was shaking my head at that bastard's sick humor as I targeted a known weak joint in the Hive ship's underbelly and fired a sonar cannon that I hoped would rattle the fucker apart. On my right, flying in battle formation, two of my battle wing pilots fired ion cannons at the same time. The brightness of the attack was almost blinding.

A cheer erupted in my communications gear when the Hive ship exploded, breaking into pieces right before my eyes. There were a few more scout ships we'd need to chase down and take out, but I wouldn't lose any more cargo ships or transport stations in this solar system. At least not for a while and never on my watch.

"Nice job, Commander." I could hear the smile in Rav's voice. "Now, get your ass back on this ship, where it's supposed to be."

"I belong out here, fighting with the warriors."

"Not anymore." The voice of my second-in-command, Captain Trist, rumbled through my head and he made no attempt to hide his disapproval.

Fuck. He was such a by-the-rules man that he had the entire regulations guide shoved up his ass.

"If I stayed on the command deck all the time, Trist, you'd be bored."

"You take too many risks, Commander. Risks you should not be taking. You are responsible for nearly five thousand warriors, brides and their children."

"Well, Captain, if I die today, they'll be in good hands."

Rav answered, "No. They'll be begging General Zakar for mercy."

"Noted. Returning to the ship now." If I were to be killed, or worse, captured and contaminated by the Hive, my father,

General Zakar, would most likely come out here and take command of the *Battleship Zakar* himself. I might be a bit adventurous, but my father was cruel and unforgiving. If he returned to active duty, the body count would double or triple, on both sides.

We worked hard to hold the Hive in place, to prevent their expansion into this sector of space. My father would try to defeat them, drive them back. The Hive response would be to send more soldiers, more scouts. Things would escalate quickly to what they'd once been. We'd managed to spread them out across multiple sectors of space, slowly weakening our enemy by denying them new bodies to assimilate while thinning their lines. My father's aggression would undo years of careful Coalition strategy, years of planning and work.

My father was too arrogant and stubborn to listen to reason. Always had been.

I had two younger brothers, both still in combat training on the home planet of Prillon Prime. They were a decade younger than I, and nowhere near ready for battle. My death would force my father out of his role as advisor to the Prime, and back into active service here, on the front lines. The alternative, to retire the Zakar name, our battleship reassigned to another warrior clan, was unacceptable. My father would rather die than see his family dishonored. This battle group had been named Zakar for more than six hundred years.

Trist would hate having his command stripped away and the people on my ship would hate it because...hell, no one liked the general. It just proved I had to stay alive. I might not be warm and cuddly, but I did the fucking job.

As commander, I was not required to fly combat missions. But sitting in the commander's chair, bellowing orders and watching other warriors die in my place was not my idea of honor. If I'd known how fucking hard it would be, I would have turned down command of the battle group. I was the youngest commander in a century, and many argued, the most reckless. The elder generals labeled me rogue. But they didn't understand. I needed to fight. I needed the rush. Sometimes, I didn't want to think, I just wanted to fight...or fuck, and since I had no mate, fighting satisfied the restless rage I carried. Even now, with the mission successful, I should have been appeased. *Eased*. I wasn't. Far from it.

Perhaps a warm, willing female with soft skin and a wet pussy could tempt me to give up these battle runs.

The Hive scouting teams had been infiltrating our space for several weeks, sending three- and six-man teams in, sneaking past our defense perimeters to surround and attack transport relays and cargo vessels. In short, they were making me look bad on the home world.

Every damn night I got a comm from my father, *after* he read the day's intelligence reports. He said he was tired of seeing my sector losing ground in this war. Fuck that.

If the uptight bastard commed me tonight, it better be to congratulate me on taking back this section of space.

My gaze shifted to the tracking monitor to my left as I turned my small fighter back toward the battleship, toward home. Yeah, the hulking metal spaceship was home. The small blasts on the screen and whooping battle cries in my ears assured me that the remaining Hive ships were being hunted down and destroyed.

I gave the command for the Seventh Battle Wing, who eagerly flew attack formation with me when I decided to charge into battle, to return with me while the other two battle wings remained to track and eliminate the rest of our enemies. Taking prisoners was not an option. Once the Hive took a man's life, we never got them back. Those who survived the Hive Integration Centers intact were lost forever, sent to The Colony to live out their final days as contaminated warriors, dead to the rest our people.

No. I preferred not to take prisoners. Death was a kindness I was more than willing to offer.

"Commander, look out!" The warning came just as the proximity alarms on my scout ship sounded. The blast of sound had barely registered when my ship was torn out from beneath me.

In a flash of bright light, the ship exploded. My body was jettisoned into the blackness of space, the flight suit I wore the only thing keeping me alive. The intensity of the explosion, the force of my ejection into deep space was worse than any whiplash, any wild ride I'd ever taken.

"Commander? Can you hear me?"

I was spinning, too fast to get my bearings, too fast to track the large, orange-and-red star that anchored this planetary system. I had no way to regain control, to stop. The pressure on my organs was painful, had me struggling to breathe, groaning as I fought to remain conscious.

"Get him out of there!"

"Another ship!"

I lost track of the number of voices as an explosion of light and heat rushed over me from my left side. Debris raced past, traveling faster than my eyes could track as the Hive ship exploded around me.

A sharp, stinging pain erupted in my thigh and I gritted my teeth as the hissing sound of my flight suit losing pressure, and precious air, chilled my blood. The suit's self-repairing system began working immediately to close the seal, to maintain life status. But I was afraid it wasn't working fast enough.

Still spinning, I closed my eyes and tried to block out everything but the rapid-fire chatter going on in my helmet. Nausea hit me, bile rose into my throat.

"He's hit, Captain. His suit is losing integrity."

"How long?"

"Less than a minute."

"Transport, can you get a lock?" Trisk asked.

"No, Sir. The explosion damaged his transport beacon."

"Who's close? Captain Wyle, what's your status?"

"Six new Hive fighters detected, heading straight for him."

"Cut them off." That was Trist.

"On it," Captain Wyle said.

"No." I groaned as Wyle then ordered his team, the Fourth Battle Wing, on a suicide run with the approaching Hive fighters.

"Damn it! Get him the fuck out of there. Now!" Trist's bellow made my head ache.

The warning alarms of my body sensors were beeping, as if I didn't fucking know my blood pressure was dangerously high and my heart rate was too fucking fast.

"Let me take a medical cruiser." That was Rav.

"No time. Wyle, get a traction beam on him."

"His suit might disintegrate under the stress." Rav again.

"It's that or let the Hive have him," Trist argued.

I decided to chime in on that one. "Fuck that," I hissed. "Wyle, do it." I'd rather explode into a million tiny pieces than end up part of the Hive's cyborg collective.

"Yes, Sir."

The energy of Captain Wyle's traction beam hit me like a brick wall, the force slamming my forehead into my helmet. Hard.

Stars danced before my eyes and I couldn't stop the scream of agony as it felt like my entire left leg was being ripped off at the knee. Explosions sounded all around, I used counting them as a means to hold on to consciousness.

When I reached five, everything went black.

———

DOCTOR CONRAV ZAKAR, *Battleship Zakar, Medical Station*

. . .

"Is he dead?" The new medical officer's voice trembled and I didn't have time to ask his name. Nor did I care.

"Shut the fuck up and help me get him out of his flight suit." The standard Coalition flight suit was made of nearly indestructible black armor, generated by our ship's spontaneous matter generators, or S-Gen, as we called them. I used a laser scalpel to cut away one sleeve before the young officer's next suggestion slammed me back to reality.

"Why don't we put him on the S-Gen pad and ask the ship to get rid of it?"

Genius. Didn't mean I had to like the little shit. "Let's move him."

I grabbed my cousin and best friend beneath the shoulders and lifted with all my Prillon warrior's strength. I could have carried him myself, but my assistant stepped forward and lifted Grigg under his knees.

He wasn't dying now. He'd done his fucking job out there in battle and it was my turn to do mine. It wasn't the time to realize if he hadn't left his command post, I'd be celebrating with the others instead of bringing him back from the fucking brink. Stupid, hardheaded fucker.

We moved him as carefully as we could to a pitch-black pad where the faint green grid-lines of the S-Gen's scanning sensors quickly went to work examining Grigg's armor, so we could remove it in stages. The outer layer of Grigg's armor had so many micro-cuts it looked fuzzy, instead of smooth and hard. Blood dripped from his left boot to hit the floor with a spattering sound that made me grind my teeth. His helmet had been warped to the point that I could not release the locks and remove it. The helmet's visor was shattered, a thousand tiny cracks obscuring my view of Grigg's face.

If the bio monitors hadn't insisted he was still alive in there, his heart still beating, I would never have believed anyone inside this destroyed armor had survived.

I placed my hand on the activation panel and ordered the ship to remove Grigg's armor. Impatient, I didn't look away as the faint green light glowed around his body.

When the light faded at last, leaving Grigg naked and bleeding on the pad and my heart stuttered.

"Fuck, Grigg. You're a mess." Grigg was covered in blood, his normally dark, golden skin a strange smear of orange and red almost everywhere. His left leg was cut through to the bone halfway between his knee and hip, blood rushing to the floor with each beat of his heart.

Dropping to my knees I placed a bleed blocker over the wound. It wouldn't heal him, but it would stop him from bleeding out while I carried his stubborn ass to the ReGen pod.

"I need more help over here!" I shouted. Aides and other techs came running.

"Help me. Careful of his leg." I lifted him, once more under the shoulders, trying to keep his head from flopping like a loose doll's. Other hands joined mine and he was quickly lifted from the table.

"ReGen pod?"

"Yes. Immediately."

We moved as a unit, shuffling quickly to the large, full-body submersion unit used for the most critical wounds.

"Shouldn't we sedate him first?"

"Shut up or get out," I growled.

"Yes, Sir."

The door to the medical station slid open and Captain Trist strode into the room, took one look at Grigg and came to a dead stop. "Is he dead?"

"No. But he will be if we don't get him into ReGen."

Trist stepped forward between two techs and helped lift Grigg under his hips. If Grigg had been an average Prillon warrior, we wouldn't have needed five of us to move him, but he was a fucking seven-foot giant. Grigg, like all members of the warrior class on Prillon Prime, was a big motherfucker at close to three hundred pounds of hard, lean muscle. Built for war, the Prillon race was bigger and stronger than almost any other race in the Coalition. And the Zakar family? Well, Grigg and I belonged to one of the oldest warrior clans on the planet. He was genetically predisposed to be one big motherfucker.

I exhaled in relief as we lowered the commander's body into the bright blue light of the ReGen Pod. The clear cover slid over Grigg's bruised and battered body automatically, the sensors beginning to work immediately. We stood back and inspected the raw burns and lacerations on his face that were clearly visible.

"He's lucky he didn't lose his right eye." The medical officer who'd assisted me moved by rote over the control panel, adjusting the settings to ensure Grigg would heal at the maximum speed his body would allow.

"He's lucky he's not dead." Trist slammed a blood-covered palm down on top of the clear casing.

He turned to me and I shook my head. "Don't look at me."

"You're his second. Family. Can't you fucking control him? He can't keep doing this." Trist's rage colored his pale yellow skin a dark gold. "He's the commander of this battle group, not infantry or a fighter pilot. We can't afford to lose him."

"He inspires the men." The medical officer on the other side of the ReGen pod spoke reverently, awe in his tone. "They talk about him in the cafeteria. Hell, everywhere. They talk about him everywhere."

"Do you need to be here?" Trist asked.

The medical officer looked at the monitoring panel. "The commander is healing properly. All protocols for his regeneration have been set."

"Do you need to be here?" Trist repeated.

"Technically, no." The young recruit looked shocked, his fear of Trist causing his skin to pale to a sickly gray nearly the same color as his uniform. With good reason. The captain was nearly as big as Grigg and twice as mean.

"Leave us."

In seconds, I was alone with the captain, who slumped into a seat on the edge of the room. "How do we stop him? It's like he's insane. Hell, it's like he's turned into a raging beast, like a fucking Atlan berserker."

Now that the danger was past, rage mixed with relief as I took a seat next to Trist where we both could keep an eye on the commander's unconscious body. Blood coated our hands, our uniforms.

"We can't stop him." Staring down at my bloody palms, I wanted to strangle Grigg. I loved him like a brother, but he'd allowed his father's rage to push him too far. He took too many risks. He was playing a very dangerous game and he was losing. He was alive, so it wasn't a complete failure, but next time? And the next? Eventually the odds would catch up to him. Next time he really might die.

I'd had enough. Trist'd had enough.

I'd given it a lot of thought, and just one solution presented itself, I just hadn't mentioned it before. There were no secrets between Grigg and me, but this one, I'd kept. Considered it. Ruled it out in the past. But now, now that he was in a ReGen pod healing a fucking severed femoral artery, broken femur, severe concussion and who knew what the fuck else, it was time.

"We'll never convince him to stop, but his mate might."

Trist straightened his legs out in front of him. "He doesn't have a mate."

Slowly, I turned to face him. "Then we need to get him one."

Trist glanced my way. "How do we do that?"

I stood then, pacing. "Right now, you are in command."

Order of succession was taught on the first day of fighting school. This was not something I had to explain to Trist. "And?"

"He's a commander in the Coalition Fleet. He's eligible to request a matched mate through the Interstellar Bride Program. Order me to process him for a matched mate. Order me to put him through the matching protocol."

Trist's eyes widened at the very idea. He didn't live life on a hair trigger like Grigg did. He thought things through, clearly and methodically.

"And when he wakes?"

I grinned. I'd thought this through clearly and methodically, too.

"The processing is subconscious. It'll be like a dream. He won't remember a thing until it's too late. He won't know what we've done until his mate arrives, in the flesh."

Trist smiled. Holy fuck, the man smiled. I'd never seen him do that before, thought his face was broken or permanently fixed in a benign gaze.

"And then he'll be too busy fucking her to care—or get into any more fucking trouble." Trist stared at me for a count of five before he burst out laughing.

I was too shocked by the sound to process his words.

"Do it, Doctor. Get him a mate. That's an order."

ommander Grigg – Private Quarters, Battleship Zakar

FOR THE TENTH night in a row, I stared at the ceiling above my bed, restless. Waiting. For *her*.

Who she was, I could not say. A goddess, perhaps? A figment of my imagination? An image conjured by my brush with death?

All I knew was my cock was hard as a rock and the softness of her skin, the tight, wet heat of her pussy chased me into my dreams until I woke moaning and sweating, forced to take my own hand to my hard shaft to ease the discomfort. It didn't take much, one stroke, maybe two, and I came like a rutting youth.

This *her* was haunting me.

Even now, during the fourth rotation, the least active rotation on the ship's schedule, when most of my people slept, I could not rest. I had not been able to rest since I woke up in that ReGen pod to Rav's frown and Captain Trist's scowl. They hadn't said a word about my recent scrape with death. They hadn't needed to. My father had ranted for two hours, until his face was bright orange with rage and I'd worried my ears would begin bleeding. Again.

"Oh, fuck off. All of you." I spoke to no one, my spacious quarters and huge bed big, though large enough to hold three or four bodies, only held me. Not that I couldn't find a woman to warm my bed if I wished. I didn't. At least, I never worried about it overmuch, until now.

When I'd been younger, on leave, I'd had more than enough female companionship to satisfy me. As I'd aged and advanced in rank, the women expected more. It wasn't enough for them to fuck a strong, young warrior. Now they looked at me with calculation in their eyes. Now, I was a Commander and I had *value*. They didn't want to fuck *me*, Grigg. They wanted to be *mated* to a Prillon Commander. They wanted status, rank, wealth *and* power.

But fucking and mating were completely different. Fucking was an impersonal few hours of pleasure. Mating was... everything.

My fist gripped my hard length, pulsing and ready for release. Using my thumb, I rubbed along the ridge with each pass. I knew how to get off and it was quick. My body tensed, my breath seized as a murky vision of *her* filled my head and my seed spurted hotly into my hand.

With my balls emptied, for now—I sighed, tossed off the covers and walked naked to the adjoining bathing room. Shit, I was hard again. Maybe there was something wrong with me. I wasn't about to go tell Rav that my cock kept getting hard at the thought of a beautiful woman. I sighed, gripped my cock again. Yeah, he'd fucking believe that. Worse, he might and then he'd laugh his fucking head off.

A hot shower might ease me to sleep, but first, I had to ease the ache that was growing in my balls once again.

Moments later, I closed my eyes and let the hot glide of

water pour over my body. I washed quickly, enjoying the luxury and quiet. We did not require water for bathing, but kept the ancient practice for one simple reason...pleasure.

My hard cock wept, a drop of pre-cum gathered on the tip. Fuck, maybe the ReGen pod had fixed me too well, given me some kind of super-cock, for I'd never been this quick to recover. Wrapping my hand around the thick head, I turned to face the water and leaned back against the shower tube as the heat surrounded me, and I tried to *remember*.

The dream. Her wet pussy. Her full, round breasts. The strange color of her skin, her strange and exotic dark eyes and black hair. She was not a golden Prillon female, but an alien woman. Strange. Beautiful. I'd held her legs open and spread her pussy lips open wide with my rigid—

"Commander!" The excited voice blasted through the comm speaker in my bathing room and I froze beneath the water. Fuck.

"This is Zakar," I growled. My thoughts of *her* were clearer this time. I recalled more details of her and the comm had stolen that vision from me, ruined the moment until she faded in my mind once more.

"Commander, there's an emergency. You're needed in med station one."

"What is it?"

There was a short silence and I pumped my cock once, twice, then growled. This time, I didn't have time to finish. I'd have to stuff my poor cock into a proper uniform and suffer the stiff, black armor squeezing my cock and balls like a vise.

"Doctor Zakar said to tell you—I can't say it, Sir."

That made me chuckle. I could just imagine what my smart-mouthed cousin had instructed the young officer to tell me. "Speak freely. What did he say?"

With a sigh, the officer answered. "He said to get your ass to medical and to fucking hurry. Your mate has arrived."

"My what?" My booming voice echoed off the walls in the small bathing room.

"He ordered me to cancel comms. Sorry, Sir." The comm unit went dead and I rinsed and dried my body, my head spinning.

My mate? What the fuck was he talking about?

A few minutes later, I stormed down the green-lined hallways to medical station one and found my cousin pacing.

"What the fuck, Rav?"

He turned on his heel, spinning at the sound of my voice. "Prime's bollocks, Grigg. You're fucking slow." Rav was tense, the lines of his neck and temples strained, his eyes glassy with excitement, or terror, I wasn't sure which. My need to offer reassurance and control, even with my warriors, settled in me and my pulse slowed as I placed my hand on Rav's shoulder and squeezed.

"I'm here. Now, tell me what you need."

Rav stood tall in his dark green doctor's uniform, closed his eyes and took a deep breath. When I was sure he was all right, I dropped my hand to my side and waited.

Rav opened his eyes, the bright sheen still there, still unidentifiable. "She's here."

"Who?"

"Her name is Amanda Bryant. She's from a new member planet called Earth."

"Who is she? Why is she here?"

"She's your matched mate, Grigg—our mate."

I couldn't breathe. The ReGen pod. The dreams. Fuck all, those dreams. My cock stirred to life. The dreams were real. She had a name. Amanda Bryant.

"What have you done?"

Rav turned away from me without answering. Instead of explaining himself, he went into a med unit and I followed, the door sliding silently closed behind us. There were a few beeps from machinery, but all of the medical techs worked quietly and efficiently. I didn't take my focus from Rav to count the number of patients, but the unit could handle three critical cases and had nearly twenty additional beds, and they all seemed to be buzzing with gray uniformed medical officers and a couple of doctors wearing green. I ignored them all, waiting for Rav's reply.

"Only what Captain Trist ordered."

I didn't believe that for a second. Trist followed the rules. Rav didn't. He'd only follow Trist's orders if I were out of commission, such as being—

Shit. Such as being half dead and unconscious in a ReGen pod.

"Conrav?"

I said his full name. I *never* said his full name.

"You were dying."

"Rav!" I snapped, making the techs jump.

"She's beautiful, Grigg," he said, his voice almost...wistful? "So soft." He stepped close to me, lowered his voice so only I could hear. "So many fucking curves. God, her pussy is pink. And her ass. Fuck, I've been ready to take her since the moment she transported. Wait until you see—"

A soft, feminine moan sounded from the other side of one of the private medical exam rooms, the sound going straight to my aching cock. My eyes widened, for I recognized that sound deep inside me. I'd heard it in my dreams. I'd come not long ago while aching to hear that sound.

Rav grinned like a child on his birthing day about to open the largest present. "She's coming awake."

Despite my irritation with Rav and Trist's interference, I was intrigued and followed a step behind the doctor as he entered the smaller exam room. "She's mine?"

"Yes. Matched per the Interstellar Bride Program's formal

processing protocols. The match was almost one hundred percent. She's perfect for you in every way."

I was fucking tired of the Coalition dictating every tiny detail of my life and wasn't sure this would be any different. There were so many protocols, all of them impeccable. As leader, I was fucking sick of protocol. That's why I had promoted Trist to my second-in-command. He loved that shit.

"Look, cousin, I know you're excited, but I doubt—"

I saw her then, my mate, my bride, and I stopped dead. Rav grinned and walked past me, gathering his medical equipment for something.

"What's all that for?" I asked, my voice filled with awe.

"For her exam and testing. I had to wait until she was awake, and for you to be present."

She was stunning. Thick dark hair lay in dark curls over the thin pillow. Her skin was not golden or yellow like a Prillon female's, but a softer, deeper shade of dark cream. She lay on her back on the exam table.

"She transported here?"

Rav shook his head. "To the transporter room, but she was transferred here."

"Like this?" I saw red, for she was gloriously naked and she was *mine*. "Who saw her like this?"

Rav's eager expression—that of being her second mate—shifted to the clinical face of a doctor.

"I was there for her arrival. I wrapped her directly in the sheet that's beneath her."

I saw the white covering that hung over the edges of the table.

"No one has seen her like this, but me."

I glanced behind me, the door firmly closed.

"That's right, Rav. No one sees her like this. Ever," I growled the last, an instinctive need to protect her rising with a speed and ferocity I would never have believed possible. My reaction was illogical, as our official mating ceremony would be witnessed and blessed by my chosen warriors, those Rav or I chose to honor with my trust during that sacred right. But they would be watching us fuck her, claim her, make her ours, not simply admiring her beautiful body.

Her face was delicate and softer than any female's I had ever seen. Her breasts were full and ripe, and her pussy, as Rav had promised, was an intriguing shade of dark pink I'd never seen before. I ached to lean down and run my rough tongue through the delicate folds, to discover her exotic taste. I wanted to wedge my shoulders between her perfect thighs and spread her open so I could fuck her with my tongue. My mouth watered at the thought.

"What type of female did you say she is?" I asked, not looking away from her. She stirred, but her eyes had yet to open. It was as if she were waking from a nap, not a transport across the galaxy.

"Earth. They refer to their race as human."

"I've never seen a female like her before." I hadn't. She was beautiful, lush, exotic. No female I'd ever seen compared.

"She's the very first bride from their world."

That shocked me enough to look at Rav. "The first bride?"

He nodded. "Yes. Earth was granted provisional Coalition membership weeks ago. The Hive expanded their scouting runs into the outer reaches, transport Zone 2."

Understanding dawned. "They were going after the warriors on The Colony."

Rav nodded. "Most likely, but they found Earth instead. Their attack forced the Coalition to make contact with Earth. Her people have been aware of other beings in the universe for just a few short weeks."

I remembered the reports now. Small planet. Purportedly beautiful, a stunning swirl of blue and white with a primitive—

"Earth was barred from full membership for being too barbaric, if I recall. They refused to unite and elect a Prime?"

Rav pulled his medical equipment closer and nodded in agreement. "Yes. Still busy drawing lines and killing each other over territory like wild animals. But if she's a little savage, I shall enjoy spanking that round ass into order."

He sounded nothing like a doctor in that moment. He sounded like a man who was seeing his mate for the first time, reacting to her, becoming eager for her, the very idea of her.

His thoughts echoed mine. But just in case the spanking Rav would give wasn't enough, I'd fill that pink pussy with my hard cock, fuck her ass until she screamed my name, fill her mouth with cum and hold her head back with a hard fist in her hair so I could stroke her lovely throat as she swallowed me down. But if we were truly matched, she would enjoy my need to control as much as I needed to govern her pleasure. She would enjoy it a little rough. A little wild. She would enjoy being dominated by two warriors.

Lust and a primitive need to mark and claim my mate erupted within me like a volcanic blast, my growl echoing through the room before I could think to hold back.

Shit. I was ruined.

My little mate's eyes opened at the sound, locking on me with a wariness and fear I did not welcome. Her eyes were unique, a dark brown that I longed to drown in. Right now, they narrowed with suspicion or wariness and I realized I only wanted to see one expression on her face—desire, longing, trust.

Desperation, as I made her beg for release.

I guess that was four expressions.

"Fuck, Grigg. Stop scaring her so I can get her medical clearance and we can—get her settled in your quarters."

I nodded in agreement, eager to get her back to my bed where we would truly claim her for the first time and enjoy the full benefits of having sealed our mating collar around her throat.

I watched my mate's expressive gaze travel from myself to Rav and back again. She noticed everything in the room, the lights, the exam equipment, the door, yet made no move to cover herself, as if the condition of her body was irrelevant.

I found her behavior odd, and intriguing.

Moving slowly so I wouldn't scare her, I stepped forward and bowed. "Welcome. I am Grigg, your matched mate, and this is Conrav, my second."

She didn't move, but did speak, and her voice made my cock impossibly harder. "Amanda."

Her name wasn't enough. I needed to hear her voice calling out my name, rough with pleasure, breaking as she begged.

She looked down at herself at last and cleared her throat. "Holy shit, all my hair is gone."

Her skin was indeed smooth and flawless, as all females' should be. I didn't answer, not sure what she might have looked like before, but very pleased with the soft sheen of her skin, the gorgeous view of her pussy.

She caught me looking, and cleared her throat. "Oh, well, no more shaving. That's a perk, right?" Her legs shifted on the exam table and I forced back the order that rose in my mind. I did not want her legs closed, I wanted them open, wide open for my cock, my mouth...for whatever the fuck I wanted.

"May I have a blanket or something? Clothes?"

I shook my head. "Not yet. Rav is a doctor. He must complete your medical evaluation first."

A little line creased her smooth brow, her dark eyebrows a stark contrast to the cream of her skin. Her face was so unlike ours, smooth and round, with soft curves and valleys I longed to explore with fingers and lips. I wanted to know what her skin tasted like, if her exotic taste would match her scent, something sweet and feminine, an unusual flower I had yet to explore.

"I was examined at the processing center." She looked around again. "On Earth."

Rav chuckled. "No, mate. The Fleet requires each new member submit to a full medical exam prior to release into the general population." He picked up a small device and checked it for readiness. I had no fucking clue what it was for.

Her dark brows furrowed and I wanted to reach out and smooth the worry line away. She turned to me. "I thought you said you were my matched mate."

I nodded once. "I did."

She looked at Rav, who bowed in reverence, as I had. "But—?"

"I am Doctor Conrav Zakar, your second mate, Amanda Bryant of Earth."

"Second mate?" Her face turned a dark shade of pink, not as enchanting a pink as her pussy, but still, beautiful. "I don't—oh, God." Her dark eyes looked everywhere but at us, her mates, as she mumbled to herself. "That dream. Shit. That dream. Oh, God. I'm such a pervert, and now what? Two of them? Shit. Robert said this job would be the perfect fit for me. See if he likes two mates. I can't do this. I can't."

4

I'D HEARD of people who freaked, who panicked in new situations. That wasn't me. I'd been compared to a chameleon, my mixed heritage and skill with language making it easy for me to blend in and adapt to any environment, any job. But no chameleon had ever been to fucking space. This...this was crazy. The two before me weren't arms dealers, assassins, Russian Mafia or even Chinese Triad. They were aliens. As in, from fucking space.

They were big. Holy hell, they were big. Like almost seven feet and built like the Samoan rugby team. On steroids. They didn't look human with their golden skin and eyes. The big one, Grigg, had dark, rust-colored eyes and light brown hair that looked like caramel coating on a sundae. They also didn't look like little green men from the sci-fi movies either. They were actually really attractive. Handsome. Rugged. Huge. And supposedly we were matched mates. Matched! Some testing process had put us—us? How the hell was I matched to two guys?—together as being perfectly compatible, perfectly right for each other.

And my *second* mate? Conrav, the doctor? He was almost as big, same sharp features and gold coloring, but his eyes were like sunlight through honey and his hair a pale gold so beautiful I had to force my gaze away.

I knew one thing about them, they were...perfectly hot. But that didn't matter because I was in fucking outer space and the one guy, Rav, was waving some blinking sensor stick over me.

I sat up, grabbed the sheet that I was sitting on—why it wasn't over me instead of under me, I had no idea.

"You are thinking too hard. According to our new data on humans, your heart rate is elevated and your blood pressure is abnormally high." Conrav spoke, his voice clinical now, the desire I'd imagined in his eyes completely gone. Which, for some unknown and completely unfathomable reason made me even more upset than being gawked at by two lust-filled alien males.

I stared at the man and swatted the stick away, grateful for whatever strange processor I now had in my brain, and the slight headache it caused, for I knew that without it, I wouldn't understand a word these men were saying. "Well, Conrav Zakar, You don't have to be a doctor to know my heart rate goes up and my blood pressure rises with what's called White Coat Syndrome."

"You may call me, Rav, mate."

"Get that thing away from me."

Rav frowned. "I am not familiar with that syndrome. Is it something that occurs on Earth? Is it infectious? It should have been eliminated by the transport system's bio filters."

Grigg laughed where he leaned against the wall, arms crossed. "I think she's telling you she's nervous, especially around doctors."

"He's right. Doctors on Earth, at least where I'm from, wear white lab coats in a hospital, like a uniform." When Rav looked at me, a little reassured that I wasn't going to spread some strange disease, I continued. "Look, I'm fine. Nervous, yes. I'm on a space ship in outer space. Until a couple months ago, I didn't even know you guys existed. And now I'm here and can never go back."

I hated the catch I heard in my voice. Tugging the sheet around me a little tighter, I sighed. Yeah, that teeny-tiny, little bit of coverage didn't help me feel better at all.

Grigg pushed off the wall and stood beside Rav. One was dark, the other fair. Grigg wore black body armor, a uniform I recognized as one of the Coalition military's standard issue for the front lines. The other wore a dark green shirt and pants. The material hugged his massive chest, and he looked intimidating and freakishly strong beneath his clothes, despite the fact that it was not as thick as Grigg's battle armor. The green had to be a uniform as well, for no guy would choose that attire otherwise.

I wondered what they would look like naked, their chests and shoulders bare for me to explore.

What was wrong with me? I'd been awake all of two minutes and I wanted to climb them like a tree monkey.

"This ship is your home now. We will be your family. Once we have your medical clearance, we can begin our new lives together," Grigg vowed.

I looked up at them and felt small. The way they were gazing at me made me feel feminine, desired, wanted. I'd never felt that way with a man before. Ever. Still, that wasn't why I was here. I needed to remember that.

"About that." I waved my finger between them. "It's the 'us' part of that sentence that I'm struggling with."

Grigg looked at Rav.

"You don't have second mates on Earth?" Rav asked.

"Uh, second mates? You mean threesomes?"

"Ah, yes. Threesomes. You belong to both of us. Soon, we will not only be mates, but we will bond in the formal claiming ceremony and our connection will be permanent."

I shook my head. "There are no permanent threesomes on Earth. It's a one-time thing. A sex thing that some like to try. For fun."

"You mean you fuck two men only for recreation, not a mating?" Rav asked.

My eyes widened and I felt my cheeks heat. "Me? No. No, no, no. I just assumed I would be matched to one mate, not two. Having two husbands, or mates on Earth is actually illegal where I'm from."

"Illegal? You are required by law to only have one?" Rav grinned and I swear they both puffed out their chests. "You will like being mated to two much better."

"Yes," Grigg added, nodding. "Two men to protect you."

"Shelter you."

"Cherish you."

They went back and forth with the list.

"Touch you."

"Fuck you."

"Taste you."

"Make you scream with pleasure."

The last was said by Grigg and with a deep, gravelly voice that made goose bumps rise on my arms.

The stick thing in Rav's hand had coils, and they began to glow bright blue. He held it up, waved it in front of me once, then grinned. "You like that idea."

I tried to scoot back on the table, but my knees hung over the footrest and I couldn't easily scoot any farther up toward the head of the table and away from him. The men, however, took a step closer. "What? No. No, no, no."

"You say no quite a bit, alien. It will be our job to make you say yes much more frequently," Grigg said, his eyes promising a thousand different kinds of erotic torture.

Oh shit, that was really hot.

"I don't like the idea of the two of you fucking me." That was a whopper of a lie, but I didn't know these men, these... *aliens* and I shouldn't be attracted to them, to the idea of the two of them positioning me the way they wanted on this exam table so they could both fuck me. Perhaps one in my pussy and the other—

The stick's light changed from blue to red.

"You will not lie to us, Amanda. Ever. What we will share is based solely on the truth. We give you this one chance to learn this, but from now on you will be honest about your needs and desires, or you will be punished. While your mouth may be saying one thing, your body—" Grigg pointed at the stick thing "—does not lie."

"That thing can't tell you what I want." Could it? Did they have freakish mind-reading gadgets, too? Or a freaking magic wand while they were at it?

Rav answered, leaning so close I could feel the heat of his body, and that heat made me shiver. "It senses all of your body's functions. Heart rate and blood pressure, true, but also your level of arousal, the heat rising in your skin, the thick rush of blood to your pink pussy."

I pushed my hair over my shoulder. "Where I'm from, heart rate and arousal levels aren't tested together, nor are they equally vital to staying alive."

"Ah, that is where we differ then. If you are not attracted to us, aroused by us, then there will be no bond." Grigg's throaty voice made goose bumps rise on my flesh and my nipples harden. God, what would it feel like to have his cock buried deep as that voice ordered me to— "Mates bond for life, Amanda. If a bond is not made, then the warriors must surrender their bride into the keeping of another, a mate able to arouse her, to satisfy her needs and earn her trust. So when a new bride arrives, it is crucial to test her ability to become aroused—to reach orgasm—to ensure there is no medical reason preventing her from feeling the expected attraction and compatibility for her mates."

My mouth fell open, and I stared wide-eyed at them, then the door. "You want to get me off and claim it all is just part of a medical exam?"

"We do not want you off anything, Amanda Bryant. I must test your nervous system and response. Then, we will fuck you, mate," Rav promised, as if I'd been complaining. "I apologize that we are unable to go straight to fucking. Per processing protocol, we must first test you with our medical machinery."

I relaxed then. They were hot and all, but I wasn't going to fuck them right now. I wasn't a slut and I refused to let them think that of me. Besides, this was a job. Just a job. I had to remember that. Yes, I'd agreed to come out here and act as an alien's mate. But first and foremost, I was a spy. My loyalty and my life belonged to my country, to my planet, to the men, women and children of Earth I'd spent the last five years of my life protecting. If they wanted to hook up some gadget that sent zingers along my nerves? Whatever. I'd probably had worse.

"How about I just tell you I think you're hot."

They glanced at each other but once more Grigg devoured me with his gaze and Rav did the talking. "Our body temperatures are the same as yours, so I do not know why you think we are over warm."

That made me smile. "Sorry, Earth slang. I think you're attractive."

Rav sighed. Was that relief in his gaze? I'd never once, not for a second, even considered that these big, bad warrior aliens would be worried about my opinion of them. Worried that *I* might not want *them*. I was the alien here. The odd man out.

I imagined their women were probably well over six-foot

tall, golden and built like world-class athletes. Me? I was average height, dark brown hair just curly enough to look a bit wild, but never styled, average C-cup breasts, too round an ass and too soft everywhere else. Perfect for being a spy and blending in. My eyes were nice, the dark brown reminded me of hot fudge on a sundae. But they were the only truly beautiful thing about me. But the rest of me was soft and boring, and I was nowhere near the size of women they must be used to.

God, and they expected me to fuck both of them? Be mated to both of them? Forever?

Oh, shit. My pussy betrayed me, pulsing with slick heat as fragments of the dream I'd had in the processing center played through my mind. Suddenly all I could think about was Grigg at my back, forcing me to take his cock, to kiss him as Rav's tongue worked its way to my—

"Well, this testing should be easy." Rav's grin was wicked and I squeezed my thighs tighter together beneath the fragment of sheet as the wand thing in his hand went crazy. "Mate, will you permit me to test you now?"

"You want to test my attraction for you?" Whatever. I already admitted it. What kind of testing could they do? They could wave a hundred of those wand things in the air, I didn't care. What I needed was to get ahold of one of them and send it back to Earth. I was pretty sure the magical wand was one of those technologies these aliens had denied us.

Rav nodded. "Yes. I must test your compatibility and attraction levels. It is protocol, Amanda. Something every bride goes through upon arrival."

I shrugged. "All right. Go ahead then."

"Good," he replied. "Then lie back on the exam table head on the pillow. Yes, like that. Now put your hands up and touch the wall behind your head. There, but closer together."

I settled on the exam table, adjusting the sheet so it covered me and pressed my hands to the wall. Odd, but fine. I could adapt. I was a chameleon.

CONRAV

THE LOOK on Amanda's face when the restraints came out of the wall and bound her wrists indicated this was not something that happened during a standard medical exam on Earth. When she started fighting the bonds, I became concerned.

"Amanda, calm yourself." I went to the side of the table and brushed her dark hair from her face. "Shh."

"I do not need to be restrained like this. Get these things off me!"

Her eyes were wide and wild.

"They are for your protection," Grigg said. "Rav is going to complete the tests and we need to ensure they are accurate. Lie still."

"What are you going to do to me?"

Grigg moved to the other side of the bed, looked down at her. His hand stroked along her bent arm. "Nothing is going to hurt."

"No more needles? I fucking hate needles. Beat me, water board me, but don't come at me with needles."

I shook my head, moderated my voice to try to keep our mate calm. Someone had beaten her? I'd ask her that later, but now, I had to calm her. "No needles."

"Only pleasure," Grigg added, although he'd never been to one of these exams before.

We continued to talk to her in soft voices and with soothing touches until she calmed. I looked at the numbers on the wall above her wrists. The restraints had sensors in them, testing her biorhythms. While her heart rate was still high, I was not concerned. Amanda had been correct, she *should* be nervous.

If I could just get her into position, what Grigg said would become true. She'd find nothing but pleasure from the testing.

Pushing a button on the wall, the table began to retract from beneath her legs, the lower third disappearing, leaving her round ass on the very edge of the table, exactly where I needed her to be. I took her slim ankle and lifted it up so her legs were elevated until the leg supports finished moving into position. Grigg had taken her other leg and followed my example.

"I do not need a gyno exam," she muttered, glancing down her body as he finished her placement for the test. "And when I do have one, I'm not fucking restrained."

"This is not a fertility exam."

"I don't understand." Amanda's chest was heaving, and it took all of my self-control not to be distracted by the rise and fall of her breasts. I ached to touch her skin, so taste her flesh. After so many years of believing Grigg would never select a mate, I was having trouble controlling myself.

"You are our first bride from Earth. In space, all matter is recycled and repurposed by the Spontaneous Matter Generators on board the ship. The implants will remove your body's waste automatically for recycling." I gently parted the sides of the sheet and let them fall back to hang down toward the floor, exposing her lush body again.

"What?" She struggled once more, pulling against the restraints that held her wrists against the wall. Her body was curved and perfect, her waist small in comparison to the wide flare of her hips and the very full, round lobes of her ass. They would be more than a handful, and I couldn't wait to spank her and watch them jiggle and sway, watch them turn a dark pink, listen to her moans of pain that transformed to pleasure as I grabbed them and spread them wide, claiming her, filling her ass with my cock.

Grigg must have sensed my distraction, for he answered her. "You will never need to empty your body of waste again."

"What!" For some reason that upset her and she pulled harder on the restraints, her breasts swaying side to side as she fought to be free.

"The wrist restraints are also sensors, Amanda, and cannot be removed until I have completed your processing." I used my calmest, most nonthreatening doctor voice. "I have ankle restraints as well, but they serve no purpose other than to hold you still. Can you remain in this position or will I need to secure you?"

She looked at me as if she would strangle me should her hands break free of the restraints. Through clenched teeth, she replied, "I'll hold still."

"Good. Nothing will hurt," Grigg said, moving to stroke her hair once again.

Amanda turned her head away from Grigg's touch and I pretended not to notice the way his hand froze in midair, unsure. Grigg was never unsure, but I felt our mate's rejection as keenly as he. The hope for an easy, uncomplicated mating shriveled in my chest into a cold, hungry thing. She was not what I had expected. She obviously did not want to be here.

I'd hoped for an eager bride, a woman to welcome us with open arms and a loving heart. I'd hoped for a bride gentle enough to calm Grigg's rage. So far as I'd seen, Amanda was nothing but fire and resistance, denial and fear, and I wondered if the bride processing protocols had made a mistake. She was the first official bride from her world. Perhaps the system needed further testing?

"Hold still, Amanda. I'm going to put my fingers on your pussy now. I need to ensure you receive the proper bio-implants."

She remained silent, her thighs tense and quivering, with stress or fear I wasn't sure which, and liked neither. I'd administered this exam to new mates for other warriors on board the ship dozens of times, always with a detached sense of duty and excitement for the warriors and their new mate. But this time, her pussy was mine. Her ass was mine. Her body, her fire, her eventual surrender? Mine.

Her legs were bent, her feet in the supports, her ass and pussy on display, and suddenly I lost all pretense of clinical detachment. She was our mate, and I wanted to make her come so badly the air around me grew thick and I couldn't remember what I was supposed to be doing. Gods, the wet scent of her musky arousal made my cock hard as iron ore.

5

 onrav

"Rav." Grigg's tone was raw with need, but fully in command. I saw his nostrils flare as he, too, scented our mate's desire.

With her head tilted away and her body tense, I would think her under duress. She'd given her permission and, as we had told her, her body did not lie. She *liked* her new position, being vulnerable and on display. It was her scent that betrayed her. It grew stronger with every passing second as if she could feel my heated gaze on her core, could sense the dark urges telling me to forgo the required exam, drop my pants and fuck her senseless. As Prillon, we were acutely aware of our mates in this way. We could scent arousal, the need to fuck, and used it to take care of our mates. It ensured a happy and sated bride.

"What? Is something wrong?" Amanda's voice brought me back from the brink and I leaned to the side so she could see my face as I answered her.

"No, mate," I cleared my throat. "My apologies. I shall begin the exam immediately."

She settled her head back on the table, still not looking at Grigg, who stood on her right with a stone-cold, expressionless guise on his face. I knew that fucking look. He was hurt, hiding it, and about to do something stupid unless I gave him something better to do. I knew he could smell her eagerness for us. But, apparently, that wasn't enough to calm him.

"Grigg, will you please hold our mate's hand? This first part can be a bit unsettling."

Both my mate and my cousin obeyed my directive, but I knew it was only because they had nothing else to occupy them. Still, Grigg's heavy grip wrapped gently around our mate's much smaller, more delicate hand and I sighed with relief when her fingers entwined with his, the creamy color a stark contrast to his darker gold coloring.

"All right, Amanda." I was in full doctor mode now. "The first insertion will be the arousal stimulator. After that will be the nerve stimulus as well as the bio-implant device that will take care of your bladder and pussy."

Amanda stared at the wall, ignoring both of us. "Sounds like fun. Go ahead and get it over with."

Grigg growled at her fatalistic-sounding response, but I caught his gaze and shook my head. It was crucial we made our mate aroused and in need. She was scared right now, newly arrived and far away from everything she knew. She did not yet understand how much she meant to us, how greatly we valued her. But she would learn. Gods, yes, she would learn. Starting now.

I placed my hand on the inside of her thigh, on the softest skin I had ever felt, and tried not to take offense when she jumped at my touch. "Easy, Amanda. I promise there will be no needles, and no pain."

She sighed and settled down and I shifted my hand lower,

toward the glistening pink pussy I ached to taste. My balls grew so heavy they ached, hanging from my body like lead stones under my rock-hard cock, but I ignored the discomfort and lifted the wand to the entrance of her pussy.

The medical device was probably cool to the touch and I nudged her core, spreading her open bit by bit until I could begin the smooth slide, pushing it deeper and deeper into her wet heat.

One of her feet lifted from the support and she arched her back. "What the hell?" She sounded angry, and confused, but the exam was a requirement of the Bride Program's processing protocols, and could not be skipped.

Grigg grabbed her foot and placed it back into the support. "Hold still, mate."

With the probe fully seated in her pussy, the soft folds of her core folded around it like layers of silk, hugging it deep. I placed both of my palms on her thighs and attempted to reassure her. "The exam is protocol, Amanda. I'm sorry you're uncomfortable. Would you prefer I summon another doctor to complete your testing?"

"No!" She gasped the word, as if shocked I would even suggest it. Thank the gods, because the idea of another male seeing her like this made me want to kill things and I doubted Grigg would even allow it. She was not yet safe, not yet ours. We hadn't claimed her, hadn't fucked her, hadn't put our mating collar around her neck or our seed in her body, hadn't made her scream her pleasure and beg us to take her. She was vulnerable, unmated, unclaimed. And so fucking beautiful I knew the moment we stepped out of the medical station, we would be challenged for her if our collar was not in place around her neck.

Grigg's grip settled on her ankle, holding her in place. Unbreakable.

"Just—just hurry up." Her pussy pulsed, clenching around

the probe at Grigg's dominant touch, her juices flowing around the blunt-tipped device where it remained buried inside her, the nerve stimulus and other pieces hanging from the end like dead weight, waiting to be placed on her body. Inside her body.

I got to business, attaching the implant insertion device over her and the clitoral stimulator atop her nub. Engaging the suction cup, I began with the lowest vibrational setting as I reached for the anal bio-implant wand and lube.

Risking a quick glance at our mate's face, I saw that she was biting her lip, panting. Her eyes were squeezed shut. Her free hand clenched into a fist and then loosened over and over as if she were counting, or fighting for control.

Worried now, I checked the bio-monitors to ensure her health and safety. She was fine, but her body temperature had risen slightly and her arousal? Gods. I looked at Grigg. "Her arousal is nearing sixty percent."

"What does that mean?" He frowned at me, confused at my awe.

"She's more than halfway to orgasm, and I haven't yet begun the testing."

Grigg's knowing smile reflected my thoughts on the matter; we were lucky. It appeared we had been blessed with an extremely sensitive, amorous mate.

All the air in Amanda's lungs rushed out with a soft whoosh of sound, as if she'd been holding her breath, fighting her reaction to us. I applied a generous amount of lubricant to the anal device, which was not much larger than my thumb, and settled it at the opening of her ass. "Have you ever had anything inside you here, mate?"

She shook her head and startled. "No."

My cock jumped at the news. This virgin ass was mine. As Primary Mate, Grigg had exclusive rights to her pussy until she became pregnant with our first child. After that, I would be free to claim her as well, to fuck her and hope my seed would take root. Until then, as her Second Mate, her ass, her mouth, the rest of her was mine. When we claimed her in the mating ceremony, Grigg would take her pussy, and I would be balls deep in this tight, pink—I placed the lubricated probe at her entrance and slowly, carefully worked it inside.

She didn't fight us, didn't make a sound as I settled the probe deep in her ass, stretching her open, filling both of her holes as Grigg held her down.

Our brave little mate fought her body's reaction but as soon as I had confirmed that the microscopic bio-implants had been inserted, I adjusted the controls over her clit and turned them up. Higher. Harder. Faster. The machine would apply suction, vibration, pressure...whatever she responded to would be applied, whatever she needed to reach a release.

She whimpered and I watched as the monitors tracked her response.

"Seventy percent. Eighty." She was rocketing toward orgasm like an ion blast shot from a cannon. In all the exams I'd done for other warriors, I'd rarely seen a female this responsive. Gods, she was fucking perfect, and so fucking hot she was about to come. "Eighty-five."

Grigg released her hand to reach for her breast, massaging, tweaking her nipple as her hips bucked off the table. She was close to climax. So close. For us. Just for us, her mates.

"Turn it off. Now."

———

AMANDA

"WHAT?"

Turn if off? Turn it fucking off? I had a huge probe thing in my pussy, another in my ass, and some kind of perverted version of a vibrating suction cup pulling on my clit like a hungry demon forcing me to orgasm as two huge, dominant men I'd never met before loomed over me like I belonged to them.

Which I guess, according to the barbaric rules of this alien society, I did. As far as they were concerned, I was theirs now. Their mate. Their property to do with as they wished, and that meant getting me off. Then stopping. I didn't want them to stop. Sure, only a minute before I didn't want them to start, but now...

"Grigg?" Rav's voice echoed my confusion.

"Turn it off."

The command in his voice brooked no argument and I felt my pussy clench around the probe in response to his power. I shouldn't be on the brink of orgasm just from hearing that rough authority, I shouldn't want to hear that voice again. But God help me, I did. I was so close, my body writhing, my pussy aching, even my ass stretched, stuffed until I was so overcome with sensation tears threatened to spill from my eyes. I was desperate, needy, weak.

I was never weak.

Rav adjusted something down there, between my legs, and everything stopped but my labored breathing, my urge to scream in frustration. I was still stuffed and hungry for more, but the vibration on my clit, the suction, came to a complete stop, leaving me on the razor's edge like the worst tease imaginable.

I bit my lip and choked back a groan of delicious pain at being denied, refusing to reveal my need beyond that one escaped sound, my weakness to these two complete strangers. I couldn't believe I'd agreed to the stupid exam in the first place. This was unlike any exam I'd ever had.

To be left like this, raw and needy, on the edge? It was

embarrassing. Begging would simply make my humiliation complete.

I. Would. Not. Beg. *Ever.*

"Asshole." That was a word I could live with. Asshole.

Grigg growled at my insult, his rough hand on my breast gently kneading me, at the same time pinching and releasing the sensitive tip over and over. "Look at me."

I closed my eyes at his command, refusing to turn my head in his direction.

"Look at me."

I shook my head, still upset to be left like this. Fragile. Needy. Open. Out of control.

Vulnerable.

A sharp slap landed on my inner thigh, hard and fast, the burn spreading through me like a tidal wave of heat that I was not prepared to take. My eyes flew open. I couldn't stop the sound that escaped my tortured body, the whimper, any more than I could stop my core from pulsing with pleasure at the bite of pain.

The monitor thing beeped again and Rav raised an eyebrow. "Ninety."

Grigg's hand left my breast to tangle in my hair and he turned my head. The added hint of pressure, of his control, made me grind my hips up, toward the suction cup, trying desperately to make it turn back on. I *needed.*

"Look. At. Me."

Unable to deny him any longer, I did, shocked to find his face inches from mine, his lips so close I could taste the scent of his skin on my tongue, a musky combination that made me hungry to taste his flesh. Our gazes locked and I saw something so primal, so aggressive in his eyes that my body froze in place, instinctively submitting to his dominance even before he spoke.

I'd never responded in such a way before. I knew alpha

males, guys who liked to control everything, but I'd been immune. With Grigg, I was far from immune. I responded, and that scared the hell out of me. And it made that beeping thing go off again, which meant I also liked it. A lot.

"Your pleasure is *mine*. Do you understand?"

I didn't. I really didn't. What kind of game was this guy playing and why did I want to join? "No."

His huge, hot hand slid from my ankle to my thigh, to the device over my clit and he removed it from my body, slowly, deliberately. "The test is over. Your pussy is mine. Every inch of your skin is mine. Your pleasure is mine. You do not come for a machine. You do not touch yourself. You only come for me or for Rav. Do you understand?"

Holy shit. Was this guy for real?

At my silence he stood, undid the button on his pants, reached inside and pulled his huge cock free. I knew my eyes must have rounded in shock at the sight as he fisted himself with his left hand, hard, squeezing a large drop of pre-cum from the tip. Grip tight, he gathered the liquid onto the finger-tips of his right hand, pumping himself in long strokes as I watched. I couldn't look away as the thick substance gathered to several large drops, which he collected.

As quickly as he'd begun, he released his cock and let it bob as he stepped forward, placing his cum-coated fingers where the suction cup thingy had been moments before. On my throbbing clit. He looked at Rav, whose expression had transformed from stunned to a knowing grin as Grigg spoke. "Are the bio-monitors on? Will the protocols be met?"

"Yes."

That one word was, apparently, all Grigg needed to hear. He circled his fingers, spreading his fluid over my clit, down lower, around the edges of the probe where it exited my body. At first I was shocked, wondering what the hell he was doing. I didn't need any lube, I knew I was dripping with my own arousal. I didn't need to be more turned on, so—

Fire exploded in my clit and I gasped, my hips bucking beneath his masterful touch as a strange heat flooded my bloodstream. My nipples hardened instantly to the point of pain. My lips felt heavy and full. My heart raced. My pussy fluttered in mini-pulses so fast and intense that I couldn't register one from the other, and still my arousal built. After the first gentle circling, he immediately began to rub me hard, slow, even slapped my clit once, just hard enough to sting, then rubbed me with his hot, hard fingers until I was whimpering.

It was completely different than the suction. It wasn't clinical at all. It was Grigg doing to me what he wanted, giving me what I needed. I just hadn't known it until it pushed me so close to the edge.

Still, I held back, feeling so dirty, so wrong. I couldn't give in. I couldn't. This was too much, too colossal a surrender of my deepest self. I couldn't just give in to these two strangers who asked too much of me, of my body.

This was worse, so much worse than being forced to come by a machine. That was clinical. This... How could I justify this lust to my boss? How was my body's craving for Grigg's touch going to help me on my mission? This was no longer a doctor's exam. This was Grigg, my mate, forcing me to submit to his touch, claiming my body as his own.

And I was breaking. My skin was coated in sweat. My breathing was ragged. My pulse was through the roof and I could barely hold on. It was just too good. Less than an hour in outer space, and I was betraying my people with this dark need trying to escape. I wanted to give Grigg what he wanted, but I shouldn't. I shouldn't.

I looked up to find Grigg watching me with complete focus. I wondered if he counted my breaths, or the speed of the pulse at the base of my throat. His fingers stilled in my wet folds and I waited, my mind blank. Lost. I lifted my hips involuntarily, wanting more. Wanting it rough. Aggressive. Wanting it *now*.

"I'm going to lower my head and suck your hard, round nipple into my mouth. I'm going to flick my tongue over that tight, sensitive bud three times before I suck hard enough to brand your flesh as my own."

Holy shit. My pussy clenched. I couldn't move. Couldn't even blink. The promise of a stupid hickey shouldn't be this hot.

Grigg lowered his head until I could feel the heat of his exhalation dancing over the sensitive tip of my breast. "After three, you will come."

I didn't have time to think or argue for he lowered his head and suckled my tender flesh as his fingers rubbed hard and fast on my clit once again. Before I could process the action, I was counting, for he'd given me permission and I wanted it so bad. It was going to be so good and I needed it *so* bad.

I couldn't remember the last time I had a man-made orgasm and not from my vibrator or my own fingers. Certainly not from a man who knew *exactly* what he was doing. If any other man gave me permission to come and was cocky enough to know I'd obey, I'd have punched him in the throat. But Grigg, I counted.

One.

Two.

Three.

The orgasm rolled me under, the release so intense, so complete that I did not know if I moaned, cried or screamed. Perhaps all three. All I knew was pleasure, fire roaring through me from head to toe as my pussy clamped down so hard on the probe filling my pussy that the pulses in my core forced it from my body.

I floated back to myself, Grigg's gentle strokes over my

abdomen and the softest kisses applied to the undersides of my breasts, my neck, like a man worshiping at an altar.

The emptiness of my pussy did not please me and I braced my feet in the supports, moving, searching for more.

As Grigg tucked his still hard cock back into his pants, Rav slowly removed the device from my ass and the moment it was gone, the restraints binding my wrists released. I was lifted into Grigg's arms like a doll, wrapped in the sheet and cradled to his chest as he sat upon the exam table. I didn't fight him, not this time. I couldn't. I had no fight left. I was putty. Jelly. Shattered.

He massaged my shoulders, my arms, my wrists. How could he be so gentle after being so demanding, so commanding just moments earlier?

I couldn't think about him or what they'd done to me. How I felt about it or even how they'd made me feel. I was too overwhelmed, too sated. My mind was a soft blur, like waking up from a wonderful nap and I didn't want to shatter that. Not yet. Reality would return soon enough.

Rav put his equipment into some kind of container, I suspected for processing, or cleaning, or whatever these aliens did with their used medical stuff, and turned to us with three strips of ribbon in his hand, two were a deep, midnight blue, and one was black.

He set them on the exam table beside us and lifted a blue strip to his neck. The strange ribbon sealed around his neck, forming a perfectly fitted collar. He held the other blue one to Grigg, who shook his head, refusing to let go of me to take it. "Put it around my neck."

Rav walked behind Grigg and placed the ribbon around Grigg's neck. Immediately, the ribbon shrank and adjusted to the thick, muscled heat of my primary mate's neck. Now, they wore identical bands.

With just the black ribbon remaining, Rav came around the table and lifted it to his palm, holding it out to me.

"What is this?" Curious, I reached for the black ribbon. It felt like warm silk, but thicker than the ribbon it appeared to be, more like the thickness of a cat's collar back home, but about an inch wide.

Rav answered. "This is your mating collar. You must place it around your neck. We cannot do it for you."

I studied the simple black strand, confused. "Why? What is it for?"

Rav lifted his knuckles to stroke my cheek and I did not flinch from the simple gesture. After the intensity of what I'd just experienced on that exam table, his gentleness was like a balm to my senses. "It marks you as ours. For thirty days your collar will be black, indicating that you are in an active claiming period with your mates. Once we complete the claiming ceremony, your collar will turn blue, to match ours, marking you forever as an honored and protected mate of the Zakar warrior clan." Shoulders back, his chest swelled with pride. "We are one of the oldest, strongest families of Prillon Prime."

Well, whoo-hoo. Mated into a house of alien nobility. "What if I don't put it on?"

6

 manda

GRIGG GROWLED, and damn my traitor pussy, it clenched hard, closing around emptiness with an ache that wasn't welcome.

"If you refuse the collar, any unmated male who sees you may claim the right to court you for thirty days."

I could take care of myself, so what was the issue?

"What if I tell him no?"

Rav sighed. "You can't, Amanda. You have been sent to us by the Interstellar Bride Program, a declared bride, a matched mate perfect for the warriors of Prillon Prime. Should you refuse us, another has the right to claim you for the thirty-day courting period. It's too late to change your mind. Any male you refuse will simply be replaced by another, and another. Death matches will be fought. Good warriors will die for the chance to court you.

That was medieval. Stupid. "Death matches? That's crazy."

"It's custom. If someone were to try and claim you, Amanda, I would fight in a death match for you. I would win."

I wasn't sure if Grigg's confidence was because of the strength of our match or the skill of his fighting.

"What happens if I have a daughter? She has to be mated when she's born? She can't go anywhere without a man? That's ridiculous."

Grigg's answer rumbled through his thick chest. "Of course not. Females are respected among us. Honored. Those born on Prillon are protected by all the warriors of their clan until she is of mating age and chooses to take a mate's collar."

"What happens if there are no more warriors left? If she's an orphan? Or a widow?"

It was a little late to be worried about the details, but I just couldn't imagine bringing a daughter into this crazy mess, ever, if she was going to be treated like property. Of course, I wasn't going to be having children. I wasn't here to be a mate. Not really. I had a job to do. I needed to remember that. I had barely finished the thought when Grigg's next words almost made me smile.

"The question is irrelevant. Any male who looks at our daughter will be eliminated."

Rav chuckled, but actually answered my question. "If all the warriors of a clan are killed, any remaining females are allowed to choose from the remaining warrior families for protection and belonging. No one is ever left alone. That is the primary reason all Prillon brides on the front lines are honored with two mates. Should Grigg or I be killed, you will have the protection and love of your surviving mate to take care of you and any children."

"And then what? I get another second mate?"

"Generally, yes. If your surviving mate is still active in combat, you will be allowed to choose another second."

I stared at the seemingly benign strip of black ribbon in my hand and forced air in and out of my lungs. I'd been so damn cocky agreeing to this assignment.

Go out into space? Sure.

Go through an alien bride-matching program? No problem.

Fool my new mate into trusting me and then send intel back to Earth? Not looking so easy.

And maintaining a clear head? Professionalism? Staying calm and in control?

As the mind-blowing orgasm I'd just experienced had proven, I was fucked. In more ways than I cared to admit.

Rav watched me closely, as if trying to read the play of emotions running through me. If they had a gadget to test my arousal level, I had to wonder if they had something that could read my mind too. If they did, Rav wasn't waving it in front of me.

He couldn't tell that I felt anger, frustration, regret. Guilt. That one shocked me. I'd known these men for a ridiculously short time and already I was feeling guilty for my inevitable betrayal. And why? Because they made me feel beautiful? Feminine? Because the orgasm was out of this world—literally—and now I was going to be a slave to my urges? An idiot who couldn't control her emotions or her body? I'd been through too many levels of hell out in the field to surrender my sense of self so quickly.

At the same time, I had two gorgeous men who obviously wanted me. They knew just how to get me off without a clit sucker thing. What woman was stupid enough to deny myself what these men could give me? Hot, holy-fucking-hot orgasms. I could get the intel and get laid at the same time. Maybe I owed it to all women on Earth to get all the threesomes I could get while the getting was good.

Rav nodded at the collar. "Your choice, Amanda, but I promise you, we won't make it out of the medical station without challenge if you are not wearing it."

"But I was only matched to you. Why would any other warriors want me?"

Grigg rolled his shoulders, as if preparing for battle. "Because you are beautiful, Amanda. And an unclaimed bride. Women are rare out here. They would be more than willing to take their chances with you, and eager to take you to bed to convince you."

Wanting to reclaim a bit of control, to push back, as they'd just pushed me on that exam table, I asked one more question. "What if I don't want to put it on?"

Rav, gentle Rav's honey-gold eyes turned a dark, dusky shade of amber. "Then Grigg and I will fight every warrior between here and our private quarters if necessary."

I scoffed at that, but Rav's face was completely devoid of humor. I twisted in Grigg's arms to see he bore the same grave expression. They were *serious.*

"A death match?" I asked.

"I am not aware of how it is on Earth, but the mating process is serious. Crucial. Elemental. We have an advantage, because you have been matched. We know that you are perfect for us," Rav clarified.

"We will kill any warriors who try to take you from us," Grigg added. "You are ours."

What, exactly, had I gotten myself into? In order to leave the room, I had to put on the collar. If I didn't, all hell was going to break loose. While I'd never had men fight over me before, this didn't sound like a bar brawl. The term "death match" seemed pretty self-explanatory and I didn't wish anyone to come to harm. I'd wear the collar, keep people alive and get to work. Perhaps get laid while I did so.

At the same time, I sensed this was important to Rav and Grigg. This wasn't me just putting on a necklace. This was a symbol of their...ownership of me. It was important to them and wearing it for false reasoning seemed to diminish that. Again with the damn guilt.

Shaking now, I lifted the collar to my neck and wrapped it around, as I'd seen them do. The ends sealed together on their own and it felt like the ribbon grew warmer, wet, as if it were melting into my skin, fusing to me—

Seconds later I gasped as my mind and body were flooded with feelings that were not my own. Lust. Hunger. A primitive urge to hunt. To protect. To claim.

Emotions and need filled my mind and I couldn't process it all. "What is happening?" I was going to vomit. The room was spinning. I was drowning. I covered my mouth with my hand.

"Breathe, Amanda. I've got you." Grigg's voice became an anchor and I clung to it desperately to still the whirlwind of emotion rolling through me as Rav spoke.

"Lock down your emotions, Grigg. You're drowning both of us."

"I can't. Not until I've claimed her."

Rav cursed as Grigg stood and marched me out of the small, private exam room into the hustle and bustle of a busy medical ward. At least ten patients and staff turned with curious eyes to track our progress as Grigg carried me through the room. I saw two others wearing Rav's green, one a male of the same race, big and golden, and one smaller female with an odd pair of gold cuffs around her wrists and long, cherry-red hair pulled tightly into a braid that fell to her hips. The patients were mostly huge warriors in various stages of undress, their black battle armor in pieces around them, bare, bulky chests heaving with pain.

I was a red-blooded woman still half-aroused after an unbelievable orgasm. I looked. I couldn't help it. I was mated, not dead.

"Close your eyes, mate. Now, or I will be forced to remind you exactly who your wet pussy belongs to now." Grigg's order made me grin, for I hadn't realized my feelings at looking at the attractive giant were sensed through the collar. I obeyed, not wanting to start trouble by staring overlong at the biggest man I'd ever seen in my life. "What kind of alien is he?"

Grigg growled as he continued walking but Rav answered, as per what I was discovering might be the usual. "He's an Atlan Warlord. They are one of the rare races whose warriors are larger than those of Prillon."

Grigg's hold on me tightened as he finally did something other than snarl. "The Atlans are fierce warriors and are in charge of all the Coalition infantry units. They fight the Hive on the ground, in close combat. That was Warlord Maxus. He has been fighting with us for seven years, and must leave soon, his fever is upon him."

"Fever?"

"Mating fever. If the Atlan warriors do not find and claim a mate capable of controlling them, they become beasts, berserker giants a third again as large as the one you saw."

"Their mates control them?"

"Yes, in a way. Their mates are the only beings capable of calming the rage of their beast. Without a mate, they lose control and must be put down."

What the hell? Put down? Like a dog? "Put down, as in killed? You can't be serious. That's cruel."

"No, it is necessary. You are not on Earth any longer. You are not even in the same galaxy. Out here we fight for survival, we fight to defend all the Coalition worlds, including your Earth, from a fate worse than death. We do not have time for jokes. An Atlan in berserker mode killed six of my warriors on my first command before I shot him dead. He was a friend, a man I'd fought with and trusted. My hesitation cost lives, Amanda. The Atlans live by a different code of honor, a strict code designed to safeguard all they fight to protect. As he lay bleeding out, he thanked me."

I tried to imagine the strength of conviction, the depth of pain, one would feel executing a friend and my heart broke a little for the warrior carrying me. There was much humanity did not know or understand about the alien warriors under whose domain we now lived. But, that was a big part of the reason I was here, to learn, to understand, and send information back to Earth.

I heard a door open and close, then another. Soon the faint sounds of others faded and Grigg was settling me on my feet. For reasons I could not explain, even to myself, my eyes were still closed as he'd ordered. His story made me sad, and made me hurt for him. He was so damn hard, so trapped by his choices, just as I was.

I didn't want to like him overly much. I didn't want to have sympathy for him either. Today was not going to be my best day to remain strong and detached. Perhaps it was the collar, perhaps I just *liked* these men. Perhaps their sense of honor and service was not so dissimilar to the veterans who served at home.

No, they weren't *men*. They were aliens. Prillon. And it didn't mean they were right. Soldiers followed orders. For better or for worse, that was the way things had always been. And these warriors, my mates, were first and foremost, soldiers. It was up to me to discover the motivations and truths behind those issuing the orders.

When my feet touched the floor, Grigg allowed the sheet to drop and pool at my feet. His arms were around me, pressing me close, holding my cheek to his chest, the loud thumping of his heartbeat oddly human and reassuring, even through the hard press of his uniform. After a few moments, he ran his hands up and down my back, tracing my curves to the apex of my ass, then back up to my shoulders as if the feel of my skin soothed him.

"Rav?" Grigg's voice was softer than I'd heard it yet, an

apology in that one word, regret in the emotional tornado my collar forced me to feel.

"Yes." That fast, the doctor was behind me, his heat like a fire at my back.

"I can't control myself."

"I know."

"Take her." Grigg shifted slightly, gently pushing me to take a step back into Rav's arms. "Open your eyes, Amanda."

I did, to find him backing away to sit in a large chair near an even larger bed. His gaze would have burned holes in me if in physical form and I realized there was a roiling of emotion building like a caldera in his chest. I sensed it, the intensity of it, through the collar.

"What are you doing? I don't understand."

I knew his cock was rock hard and desperate to fill me. I knew he wanted to touch me so badly he was afraid he would hurt me if he did so. He was afraid, afraid to lose control, afraid he would be too rough and frighten me. As he stripped naked, the massive muscles of his chest and back made my mouth water.

Rav wrapped his arms about me and I wasn't sure if his hold was to keep me from escaping or because he wanted to feel me. He held me pressed to him, my back to his chest as Grigg stepped free of his pants, kicking them aside, his huge cock straining to reach me. It was swollen and thick, the blunt head so wide. An artery pulsed up the bulging length. I saw the drop of pre-cum on the tip, watched it slide down the smooth crown. I licked my lips, unable to stop myself from imagining what that little pearly drop would taste like burning down my throat and into my belly, or rubbed over my breasts. And it was like fire. The liquid had heated my clit somehow and I knew that it would do the same to the rest of me.

Rav's hands rose to cup my bare breasts and Grigg, watching every move, shuddered.

"Yes, Rav. We will claim her now. Fuck her. Do exactly what I tell you," Grigg growled.

Through the strange link forged by our collars, I felt Rav bristle at Grigg's high-handed demands. The collars were a powerful and heady tool. I sensed things, *knew* things I shouldn't, having just transported. Somehow, I knew that Rav was used to taking orders from his commander and would do as he said, even fucking me. It was an easy order, for he was too eager to touch me to refuse. The cock pressing hard and thick into my back told me that he was more than ready to do anything Grigg wanted him to. We were both at Grigg's mercy —I, certainly, was at both of theirs—at his whim, and for some reason, that thought made me so fucking hot I began to shake.

Grigg settled back in the chair, his knees spread wide, his cock at attention, and his arms spread across the armrests like a king sitting atop his throne. The king spoke, "Lift her and carry her to the edge of the bed. Lay her down on her back so that her head is hanging over the edge. I want her looking at me."

I didn't fight Rav's hold as he lifted me and settled me on the giant bed. The bedding was soft and a deep blue just a shade lighter than my mates' collars. Rav positioned me on my back, as ordered, my head hanging down over the edge where I had to look past Grigg's cock, up to that enormous, muscled chest to his golden face. In the dim light his eyes looked nearly black as they devoured me, lingering on my breasts where they thrust up into the air. When his gaze met mine, I shuddered at the intensity of the lust flowing through me from my men.

God, I loved the collar. I knew, just *knew*, how much my men wanted me. This wasn't a game. This was...primal.

Grigg's grin was pure cocky male, and I studied his face, this man I'd just met and was about to give myself to.

"Do you like it when I watch, Amanda?"

What? I'd never! I'd never admit it to him. "No."

"Does it make your pussy wet?"

"No." What did he want from me here? I was already naked, on my back, at their mercy. Now he wanted me to tell him I wanted him. Tell him I wanted him to watch like some pervert? No. No way. I knew Rav was kneeling at my feet, waiting, anticipation making both of us struggle to breathe.

Grigg's gaze narrowed. "Do you want us to stop?"

Shit. No. No I didn't. I wanted this, whatever it was. I'd never planned on having two mates, never planned to be dominated so completely. It disturbed me, how badly I wanted this. But I was too far gone to stop. I was here, in space. And these men were mine. Fucking mine.

"I can sense the lies through the collar, Amanda. Your mind may try to refuse, but your body will never lie to me or Rav. You've lied once. You shouldn't do so again. I will ask again, do you want us to stop?"

I felt their power, their need, their strength, their arousal through the collar, which meant they could sense mine. I couldn't hide. I could bare my body but the collar bared my soul. I licked my lips, uttered the words I could deny no longer.

"No. Don't stop."

Satisfied, Grigg held my gaze as he issued his next order to Rav. "Spread her legs and tell me if her pussy is wet."

manda

Rav's hard hands went to my bent knees, forcing them wide until my thighs were nearly flat on the bed. I was limber, and suddenly very grateful for the rigorous physical workouts that never quite took off the extra weight, but kept me limber and ready for—

"Oh, God."

Rav's tongue went deep in my wet pussy and my back arched off the bed. Holy shit, no man should have a tongue that thick—that long. I raised my head to watch him.

"Look at me." Grigg's order made my pussy clench around Rav's tongue and both of my mates moaned as my arousal flooded the connection forged by the collars. Rav's tongue stroked me inside and out, teasing my clit, then fucking me deep. The surface was rougher than any man's who had ever tasted me before, rough and expertly wielded.

He stopped and his words made Grigg raise an eyebrow. "She's so wet her cream coated my tongue like wine."

"Taste her again, Rav. Lick and taste her until her legs are shaking and her pussy swells to squeeze your tongue."

Rav went back to my pussy and I quivered, biting my lip to keep the cries of pleasure from escaping. Dropping my head, I looked up at Grigg where he watched me squirm, the eye contact driving me higher. I shouldn't enjoy the hunger of his gaze. I shouldn't be so fucking hot at the idea of him watching Rav fuck me with his tongue, but I was. I knew if this went on much longer I would beg him to take me. Beg him to touch me. I felt like a pervert, a very naughty, naughty girl.

"Suck her clit, Rav. Tease her, but don't let her come."

I shook my head in denial of his order because I wanted to come *so* badly, but couldn't tear my gaze from Grigg's intense stare as he watched me. He noticed everything, every little thing. I felt like he was getting inside my mind. He noticed when Rav's tongue hit a sensitive spot, making me jump. He watched, his scowl deepening when I closed my eyes for a moment too long. Every pulse of my empty core made me moan in pain, my arousal so acute that the folds of my pussy ached, too plump, too full. The soft sheets at my back were an erotic glide, softer than silk over my skin, but that was the only sensation I was allowed beyond Rav's mouth on my clit.

I was empty. My skin bare. Other than Rav's skilled tongue, no one was touching me.

I wanted to be touched. I needed it, needed the connection with another being. I felt like I was floating. Not real. I began to feel lost. Overwhelmed.

"Fuck her with your fingers, Rav. Make her come. Hard." Grigg's words elicited a growl from the man between my legs as what felt like three fingers spread me open, fucking me in time to the rough tongue working my clit.

Hands settled on my shoulders, holding me down. Grigg. I

hadn't heard him move. The pressure of his hands kept me in place. I couldn't go anywhere. Couldn't escape. I was trapped. Locked between them and so aroused my brain shut down. I felt like an animal, a wild mustang being broken.

"Look at me, Amanda. Look at me when you come."

I hadn't realized my eyes were closed. I opened them and immediately my gaze locked with Grigg's, with my mate's.

He leaned forward, watched my chest heave, my thighs shake. My lower back arched off the bed and I lifted my hips in an effort to escape the mouth and fingers driving me to a place I'd never been before. It was too much, too intense. I couldn't take it. I was going to explode.

"It's... I can't... Oh God—"

Rav snarled at me, his animal intensity striking me through the collar as he followed my every shift and writhe. Grigg's hold tightened. No escape. My body was trapped.

"Come, Amanda. Now."

My mind—my body had long since become theirs—was gone, held in the authority of Grigg's overwhelming control. Grigg's command triggered something in me so dark and needy that I lost all sense of self, my body responded to him instinctively and I screamed as I came apart.

Grigg held my gaze as I shattered, he was my anchor as his desire, his need drove me higher. When the orgasm tapered, lessened, then ended, I wasn't calm. I wasn't replete.

I was out of control. Whimpering. Begging. I wanted them to fuck me, claim me, make me theirs. I needed more. My body was spun up higher than it had been just moments ago, on the verge of another orgasm just from the soft slide of Rav's fingers in and out of my wet core, the soft rumble of his satisfaction as he gently licked my clit, sipping at me like I was the finest wine.

I didn't want soft or gentle. I wanted rough, hard, fast. I wanted them to fuck me. Fill me. Own me.

"Now," I begged.

Grigg's hands moved to his cock, wrapping around it with a tight grip, stroking it. His massive body was coiled like a predator about to strike. Instead of freaking me out, it made me hotter. I wanted him. Now. Right fucking now.

"Fuck her, Rav. Fill that pussy with your hard cock."

Rav's shock was like a jolt of electricity through our link. "What?"

"You heard me."

I held Grigg's gaze as I felt Rav's confusion blossom via the collar. "I'm her second, Grigg. You are the one to fuck her. Her first child is yours by right." Rav's protests caused Grigg to stand taller, to tower over me. For the first time, he looked away from me to his second.

"Fuck her, Rav. You are mine, like she is mine. Your cock is mine. Your seed is mine. If she carries our child, it will be a child of the warrior clan Zakar. Fuck her. Fill her. Now."

Rav's shock burned away, replaced by lust, longing, heat and a strange loneliness that made me gasp, the intensity of his need breaking down walls in my heart I had no intention of ever letting anyone touch. I reached for him with both hands, I couldn't help it. "Rav."

His body moved over mine, pressing me deeply into the mattress, his cock nudging me open as his mouth claimed my lips.

"Fuck her. Fuck her hard." Grigg was pacing the edge of the bed now, watching. Waiting, like a predator ready to strike, to have his turn at his prey. His satisfaction humming through my body caused me nearly as much pleasure as the hot, hard chest pressed to mine, the lips claiming my own.

Rav shifted his hips, his cock pressing forward, nudging at my entrance. So fucking huge that my pussy lips parted, opening wide around him. I tore my mouth from his, my neck arching back as I struggled with the sensation of him slowly filling me, spreading me open to the razor's edge between pleasure and pain. I squirmed, shifted my hips to adjust to his size.

"Take him, Amanda. Lift your hips. Fuck him. Take his cock into your wet pussy. Wrap your legs around his hips. Open up. You can't keep us out. You belong to us. You can take him. Fuck him. Claim him. Mark him, mate. Let him in."

This was so messed up. I couldn't sort through the roil of emotions choking me. Mine. Rav's. Grigg's. Everything was a jumbled mess of longing, lust, desire, loneliness, need.

It was the need that tore me to pieces. Theirs? Mine? I had no idea and didn't care as I wrapped my legs around Rav's hips and tilted my pelvis, giving him the angle he needed to fill me in one slow thrust of his hips.

I welcomed the stretching, the pain that soon faded to mind-numbing pleasure. It had never been like this before. *Never.*

"Fuck her, Rav."

Rav's hands tangled with mine, palm to palm, fingers entwined as he pressed me flat to the bed. He kissed me again, his tongue plunging deep as he lifted his hips and thrust so perfectly into me over and over in an increasing rhythm that made me moan as my orgasm rose.

I was on the brink, riding the edge, one more. One more.

"Stop." Grigg's order made me cry out a protest, but Rav stopped, his cock buried balls deep in my pussy. I needed him to move, damn it!

"No." My protest was breathy and weak, and Grigg had the audacity to chuckle.

"Don't worry, mate," he replied. "We're going to take care of you."

The dark promise made my pussy clench and Rav growl. Sweat dripped from his brow and onto my breast. He was close to coming as well, this delay almost impossible for him, too. "What do you want, Grigg?"

"Roll onto your back, but don't let your cock come out of her pussy."

In seconds, Rav had rolled to lie beneath me, his cock filling me even more from my new position on top of his hips and I gasped. I had to place my hands on his chest for balance, the hot feel of him almost burning my palms. Unable to resist, I ground my clit down on his hard abdomen, let my head fall back, my eyes close with abandon. So close. I was so fucking close.

Smack!

Grigg's hand landed on my ass with a sharp bite of pain and I jerked in shock, the feel of it flaring to heat and my movement driving Rav's cock deeper so that my shocked gasp turned to a moan. "What are you doing?" he growled.

I turned my head to find Grigg beside me, his arms crossed. "I—"

"Hold her down, Rav. Keep your cock inside her, but don't let her move."

"What?" I cried. "Are you...are you always this bossy?"

Rav's arms wrapped around my shoulders and he pulled me down so that my chest was pressed flat to his. I looked down at him, saw the corner of his mouth tip up. "By bossy, I assume you mean commanding. Yes, he always tells people what to do."

His huge arms were like steel bands around my back, his cock filled my core and my ass was sticking up in the air, vulnerable in a way that I realized I wasn't so sure I liked. I was reassured by Rav's words that Grigg was this dominant by nature. I also felt that Rav was powerful enough in his own right that he would protect me from harm, even from Grigg, if needed.

"What...what are you doing?" I asked Grigg, my words escaping with each quick pant of my breath. "Why...why did you make me stop?"

Grigg raised an eyebrow. "You lied to me, mate. You like it when I watch. You like what we are doing to you. I believe you were told that if you lied to your mates, you would be punished."

My brain was in such a fog of lust that I had to work for nearly a minute to recall the conversation we'd had in the medical station. Lying to my mates was forbidden and would earn me a... "You can't be serious."

Grigg's response was to spank my ass.

"Grigg!" I cried. The sting of it morphed hot and bright.

He spanked me again.

And again.

Smack.

Smack.

Smack.

"Grigg!"

Fire spread through my sore bottom as he continued to spank me and the more I tried to shift away, the harder I ground down on Rav's cock until the heat of the spanking and the pain-edged feel of Rav's hard length filling me pushed me toward another orgasm faster than I could cope with or understand.

I gripped Rav's shoulders, my fingernails digging into his skin.

The first flutter of release made me whimper, but that fast Grigg's hand was buried in my hair, angling my head up so I looked at him. "No. You are not allowed to come yet, mate. Not yet."

"What? I don't—" His words shut my body down and I sobbed with need. "Please."

He ran a gentle hand down my back, walking away to get something from one of the drawers across the room before returning. Every second felt like an hour. Rav's chest heaved beneath mine as he, too, felt the strain of holding back.

I glanced down at Rav, hoping he'd help me understand Grigg. "Shh," he crooned. "He knows what you need."

I had to doubt that, but when Grigg knelt on the bed behind me and placed his hands gently on my ass, I sighed in relief. Maybe Rav was right. Maybe Grigg did know what I needed, but he was just awfully slow about it.

Seconds later, I was squirming again as he rubbed the same warm oil I remembered feeling in the medical station into my other hole.

"Wait!"

Smack!

"Hold still, mate. I am inserting a small training device into you here, so that when Rav and I claim you together, you will experience nothing but pleasure as both of our cocks fill you."

God, the dream again. Two men. Filling me up. Making me—

"Ahh—" I squirmed at the awkward feel as Grigg worked the device inside me. As he'd promised, it wasn't huge, but with Rav's thick cock deep inside me, I felt impossibly full. Too full. It was too much. "I can't...it's—"

"Rav." Grigg's one word made Rav shift his hips beneath me, grinding his hard body against my clit. Oh yes, that felt so good.

"Squeeze his cock, Amanda. Squeeze him until he comes." I was beyond asking for anything. Beyond begging. Beyond even thinking about how intense and dominant Grigg was. I was completely at their mercy. If I wanted to come, I would do as Grigg said. I wanted it and perhaps it was because of the collar, but I knew that Grigg was giving me only what I could take, what I *wanted* deep down. Perhaps so deep I didn't even know it myself.

I lay still on top of one mate as the other stroked and played with the plug filling my ass, and I obeyed. I squeezed my inner muscles around Rav's hard length, released, over and over until his heartbeat raced in my ear and his body tensed beneath me. Rav's ragged breaths were a dark rumble.

"Come, Rav," Grigg commanded. "Now. Fill her up with our seed."

Grigg kneaded my ass, pulling my pussy lips open wider as Rav came with a shout, his cock jerking and coating my insides with his seed.

I was expecting the fire, that blissful heat of it, for there was some strange chemical in their seed that was absorbed by my body. I expected it, as I'd felt it before in the medical room when Grigg had touched my pussy with his pre-cum-coated fingertips, but could not control my reaction.

I exploded and nothing anyone did or said could have stopped the eruption of bliss that rolled through my body. I was afraid my heart was going to explode, afraid I wouldn't survive the intensity. I cried out, shut my eyes and tensed every muscle in my body. I succumbed, gave myself over to it.

In the middle of it, I was torn from Rav's arms, lifted off his cock and dragged down to the edge of the bed, my hips pulled to the edge. Still on my stomach, Grigg spread my knees wide and knelt behind me. In one smooth stroke—his path eased by Rav's seed—he filled me with his huge cock. My orgasm hadn't ended and my body rippled around his thick length and milked him.

His hands on my hips were rough, hard, urgent as he pulled me backward for each thrust of his hips. I met him stroke for stroke, pushing back to take him deep. "Yes!" I cried, needing more and more, whatever he could give.

"Touch her clit, Rav. Make her come again." Grigg was nearly breathless, but his words were clear and Rav immediately moved down the bed. He lay on his back, his face inches from mine, his long arm sliding between my body and the bed to find my clit and stroke me as Grigg fucked me from behind. Whatever he put in my bottom was pressed deeper with each stroke, his pelvis bumping the flange that kept it in place.

Rav looked dazed, shell-shocked and I knew the feeling. I had no intention of reaching for him, but I did, pulling his mouth to mine, kissing him with every ounce of desire in my body. As Grigg fucked me hard and rough from behind, my kiss was sensual and tender, an exploration and gentle claiming of my own.

I was shocked as my body spiraled higher once more. Rav's seed was a fire in my blood. The sensation of being filled in both holes? Four hands on my body. Two mouths on my skin. Everything combined to push me over the edge again.

I'd never felt like this before. Wild and untamed, uninhibited. The orgasm was unlike any other. *Nothing* had ever felt like this. Through the collar I felt their own desperate need to come and it only amplified my own. It was a swirling circle, lifting the three of us higher and higher.

Grigg roared as my pussy clenched around him like a fist, his seed pumping into me like pouring gasoline on a fire, and my orgasm went on and on until, at last, I collapsed on the bed. Grigg's cock still filled me, his hard body settled, a welcome weight over my back.

We lay like that for long minutes, all three of us struggling for calm, for breath. Rav's hand stroked my long hair. Grigg petted my sides, his hands gently stroking me from the undersides of my breasts down to the sides of my thighs, his lips tracing the bumps of my spine up and down my neck.

I closed my eyes and let them have me. We all ignored the tears that leaked from my closed eyelids. I was empty. Used up. I'd given them everything. *Everything.* And now I was torn in half. They'd seen every dark depth of me, knew me in a way no one had ever glimpsed before. I was open and exposed. Vulnerable and weak to them.

And in that moment I realized just how screwed I was. It

would be all too easy to fall in love with my mates, to want this fairytale life they appeared to be offering. And the longer I lay between them, feeling wanted, desired, and precious, the more I realized that betraying them would break something inside me.

And yet, I could not turn away from my duty to my people. I had to find out exactly what the Hive threat entailed and get as much information back to Earth as possible. Leaving humanity in the dark and at the mercy of the Interstellar Coalition wasn't an option, no matter how mind-blowing the sex with my mates.

Wasn't I just the bitch?

rigg

I DIDN'T SLEEP. Instead I lay awake all night long watching them sleep, wrapped around each other, wrapped around me.

Amanda, my beautiful mate, slept naked with her head on my shoulder, her leg entwined with mine, her arm across my chest. Even in sleep she turned to me. The sight caused hope to flare in my chest, hope that she might be my true mate, that she might learn to love me.

Her back was to Rav, his body wrapped around her from behind in a protective hold I couldn't help but approve of. His arm was long and his hand came to rest on my chest as well, his fingers lightly wrapped around her wrist, holding her even in his sleep. His touch did not alarm. He was mine, as well, and I could not have chosen a better second for my mate. He was a proud warrior of our clan, highly intelligent and fierce when needed. He would be an excellent mate for our Amanda, and with rank as a senior officer in medical, the risk that our mate would be left unprotected by two warriors' deaths in battle was small. If I died in my next raid, he would care for her, love her, fuck her—

The thought made something dark and needy twist in my gut, something that raked my insides like claws, making my soul bleed and ache and want. A sense of inevitability settled over me like a dark storm, the feeling of foreboding I'd carried all my life. My father was right. I wasn't fit to command. I was weak. Sentimental. My mind clogged with emotion and needs no true warrior dared carry. I hadn't realized they even existed until now. Until Amanda.

Unable to stave off the pain, I pulled free of my mates' arms and legs and slid silently from the bed.

Damn Captain Trist and his meddling. There was a reason I had not requested a mate. I didn't expect to live long enough to claim a woman and make her my own. Rav had always known he would by my second, but I'd made it clear to him many times that if he wanted to request a mate of his own, as Primary, he should do so. He had the necessary rank and status to qualify for a bride. There were a number of warriors who would be honored to be his second.

He refused. We'd sworn an oath to one another when we were merely boys that we would never abandon one another, and we'd remained true.

Often, it would have been easier for me if Rav had abandoned me and my stubborn ways. I wanted him to be happy, but was grateful that his loyalty was now and had always been unyielding. Truth be told, I'd come to rely on his keen mind and calming influence more than I cared to admit.

And still, I'd waited, more focused on the possibility of dying than of living, of having a life, a family. I didn't want him to mourn my death. I didn't want a mate to mourn my death. I didn't want—

Amanda. She sighed softly and shifted on the bed, reached

for me in her sleep. When her arms came up empty, she turned instead to Rav, rolling so that her forehead and nose were pressed to his chest, his arms around her in a protective cage as she snuggled deeper and went back to her dreams.

She was unexpected, as was my reaction to her. Everything about her was perfect. I couldn't stop admiring her strange dark hair or her softly rounded hips and thighs. The lush cushion of her abdomen and full breasts. Her lips, pink and kissable, just like her pussy. I'd nearly lost myself in her dark eyes as Rav made her come, as her pleasure rolled through her and they both surrendered to me, to my control. The more I demanded, the faster she melted, so submissive. I'd sensed it in her, knew through the collar that she wanted it. No, *needed* it, just as strongly as I needed to dominate. So fucking perfect for me.

Even more of a shock was the fierce need I had to control Rav, to direct him, to own him as completely as I owned my mate. I did not want to fuck him, but I needed to own him, control him, protect him and take care of him. The need roared to life from nowhere the moment our mate was between us.

He was mine and I couldn't understand the ferocity of my instinctive need to make sure he understood and accepted my dominance, my protection just as clearly as Amanda. Suddenly I was irritated that Rav's belongings were still in his private quarters, and not here, with me and our mate, where they were supposed to be. I fought the odd urge to wake Amanda and talk to her, to ask her about her life and give her a tour of my ship, to show off like a young upstart trying to impress a woman, not a commander who needed impress no one.

Instead of worrying about my command, the scout missions, battle strategy, I sat in the dark like a fool staring her beauty. I counted her breaths, fighting the urge to wake her and take her again, slowly. I imagined kissing her lips, tracing her flesh, learning every curve and dip and hollow, the sensitive places on her skin that would make her melt, or pant, or come. I sat alone in the dark wondering if my mates had what they needed to be settled, content, happy. Wondering if I would be enough for them. I needed to be enough.

And I never fucking needed anything. I didn't do entanglements. I battled Hive cyborgs. I fucked for pleasure. I fought next to my warriors to quiet the rage in my blood, to fight back the abyss of anger that threatened to drown me every time I spoke to my father or watched another warrior die in battle. And yet that all quieted when I was deep inside Amanda, when I made her come, when I filled her with my seed.

Staring at my mates, something raw and ravenous stirred to life within me and I feared nothing would calm me now.

I felt like an alien in my own skin, a stranger with thoughts and desires I did not recognize and could not control.

Brooding in the dark was not something I enjoyed, so I rose and quietly cleansed my body in the shower unit. As I settled a fresh uniform on my shoulders, I felt the weight of command, the responsibility settling me in a way nothing else ever had, in a way completely different than I found with my mate. This was familiar, normal. Comfortable.

I was on the command deck five minutes later, my mind blissfully empty of longing, need, desire and confusion as I poured over scouting reports, talked to my best flight captains about imminent battles. They noticed the collar about my neck, but were wise not to mention it. Not when we knew there were more pressing matters than my taking a mate.

The Hive would come. The Hive hunger for more bodies to convert, for more raw material for their Integration Centers, was insatiable. They consumed all life, it was their means of existence. And my battle group was on the front lines, so close to the Hive central command that we often fought two or three times as many battles per week as other sectors.

Always before, that thought filled me with self-importance.

We were in one of the oldest and deadliest sectors of the war. My father had seen to that, his expectations for his son the only thing bigger than his pride in the Zakar clan's warriors. Battle Group Zakar would never relocate, never back down. Our clan had fought here for hundreds of years.

"Commander, the comm." My communications officer spoke from her position at the comm panel.

"My father?"

"Yes, Sir."

Great. Just what I didn't fucking need right now. "Patch it through to the Core." The Core was my personal nickname for the standard-size meeting room found on every ship. The private space was designed for meeting with top officers to discuss strategy or ship's business. It was where I met with my captains, disciplined my warriors and made battle plans.

I left the command deck and walked to the meeting room. Seconds after the door slid closed behind me, my father's dark orange face filled the screen near the far wall. I had inherited his eyes, but the rest of me, the golden shade of my skin, was due to my mother. His coloring was passed down from the ancient lines, and he'd always believed me less for not carrying his much darker hue.

"Commander." He never called me by my name, only my rank, as if I weren't his son. Only a soldier. "I read the most recent report."

"Yes, Father. The Hive has been eliminated from that solar system."

"And you nearly killed."

And, here we went again... "I'm fine."

"Damn it, boy. You were weak today. An embarrassment. I'd advise you to spend some time in a basic flight simulator before you fly with another battle wing. You can do better than that. You are a Zakar. I won't have women giggling and twittering on about how you got shot out of your ship and floated in space like so much garbage."

"Sorry to disappoint you." His father's rant continued for several minutes as he described, in great detail, the sympathetic looks and concerned questioning he'd been forced to endure at the Prime's palace this evening. I rubbed the back of my neck, doing my best to ignore the tight ball of rage that spun and whirred in my gut every time I was forced to look at the man who had sired me.

"Don't let it happen again. You are a Zakar."

He didn't bother saying goodbye, or asking how I felt. He didn't care. He expected me to survive, to do better, to live up to the family name.

For years I'd listened to his tirades. They hadn't made my pulse race or my heart ache for a very long time. Not since I was still in the academy had I allowed my father to upset my emotional equilibrium. But tonight I sank into the nearest empty chair at the conference table and placed my head in my hands.

Hate. Rage. Anger. Shame. Love. They twisted and churned in my chest until I couldn't breathe.

———

CONRAV

AMANDA LAY IN MY ARMS, her breath a caress of heat across my chest. Her head was tucked under my chin, her naked body pressed to mine as I held her.

My mate.

I'd waited for her for years, prayed to the gods that Grigg would one day be ready to summon her, to claim her.

I was a senior officer. I was eligible for a bride of my own, but every time I considered the option all I could see was Grigg lost and truly alone. He was not my brother by blood, but he was a brother by choice and I could not abandon him in this any more than he was able to walk away from a wounded warrior on the field of battle.

The agony racing through my body was his, the new connection with our mate, the emotional ties of our collars, broadcast Grigg's pain as clearly as if he stood next to me, breaking into pieces.

In seconds our mate stirred as well, her quick intake of breath and the hand that fluttered to cover her heart proof that she felt his pain as well. Our bond was strong, stronger than I would have believed possible after just one claiming.

"What's wrong?" Her voice was a whisper and she tensed, but did not pull free of my embrace. "Grigg."

"Yes, Grigg." I sighed, kissing our mate on the forehead and reluctantly releasing her to roll out of bed. "If I had one guess, I'd say he just spoke to his father."

She sat up in bed, gloriously naked and so beautiful I couldn't tear my gaze from her flesh even as I stumbled to pull on my discarded uniform.

"His father?" Amanda pulled the blanket up to cover her breasts, her dark hair a wild tumble falling past her shoulders. Even Grigg's pain was not enough to prevent my cock from rising to attention at the sight.

"General Zakar. He's on the Prime council."

"But—" She rubbed at her chest, as if she were truly in pain. "I don't understand."

Dressed now, I walked back to the bed and leaned down to place a gentle kiss on her soft, pink lips. Gods, she was so exquisite, and mine. Mine and Grigg's, and right now that asshole needed me. "Go back to sleep, mate. I'll take care of it."

She watched me leave with a bite of anger in her eyes, fire that I welcomed. She was going to need it if she were to survive this mating between us. Grigg had become volatile, his need to control both excited and terrified me. I had no qualms fucking our mate to Grigg's exact specifications. The fact that he'd ordered me to fuck her, to fill her with my seed—and first— had been a shock, an honor so great that I'd never once ever even imagined a scenario where our firstborn child would truly belong to both of us. We would have no way to know, now or ever, who truly fathered any of our children. The honor and generosity of that act humbled me, even as Grigg's dominant behavior toward me caused a jumbled mixture of acceptance and confusion in my mind.

He'd always been brash, impulsive, arrogant and a bit wild. I'd loved that about him, been on many adventures, fought beside him in many battles. But I'd never shared his bed, never shared a woman and felt his absolute need for control. He'd never extended his iron control to me, and I was shocked to discover that I found it—stimulating. Fuck, our mate certainly enjoyed it as well.

I found Grigg exactly where I expected him to be, in the Core, his one true sanctuary. Alone.

Motherfucker was always alone.

He didn't look in my direction as I entered. A work pad lay flat and untouched on the table before him, filled, I was sure, with a hundred reports, requests and items that required his approval. He sat at the round table and looked at none of it, his gaze cold and empty as he stared at a monitor filled with the deep emptiness of space just outside our ship. If I couldn't still feel the pain and anger coming through my collar, I might have believed his façade. He'd become very good at hiding his true self.

"I'm guessing your father was his usual charming self?" I took the seat to Grigg's right and waited. "How is he today?"

The silence stretched for long minutes, but I didn't push,

just put my feet up on the table, my hands behind my head and waited for the explosion.

"Get your fucking feet off my table."

"That good, huh?"

"Rav."

"Let me guess? He broke down into tears, so worried about your wellbeing that he couldn't speak over his sobs."

Grigg snorted. "You're an asshole."

I stretched, feeling both exhausted and exhilarated by our time spent with Amanda. After what we'd done with her, I was surprised at how quickly he'd returned to his tense old self. Maybe if I could get Grigg to calm the fuck down, we could go back to our room and pull the blanket from her soft, warm body and—

"Stop thinking about our mate. You're fucking up my rage."

"So, your father. Let me guess? Your near-death experience was a blight on the Zakar name and the women at the palace are fawning all over him with their concern for the infamous Commander Zakar."

"That about sums it up."

"You tell him about our mate?"

"No."

"What? He didn't notice the collar?"

Grigg shook his head. "He only sees what he wants. The rest..."

"So you didn't tell him. Why not? Maybe the women would leave him alone if they knew they had no chance of claiming you."

"They never had a chance."

"They didn't know that. I'm sure you're number one on so many mothers' potential mating lists for their daughters that you are practically a household name back on Prime."

His silence stretched and I let it ride, giving him time to come to grips with what I'd just told him. He was a brilliant warrior, but when it came to politics or women, he had about as much finesse as his father. A fact to which I would never enlighten him.

"I'm not going to tell him about her."

I frowned. "Why not?"

He finally looked at me, and I was relieved to feel the tension coiling through our link calm as well. "I like the idea of him suffering their attentions. I might never tell him."

"Fine. I don't care about your asshole father. I care about Amanda. What are we going to do about her?"

That narrowed his attention. "What do you mean?"

"Didn't you feel it when we were finished with her?"

"Feel what?"

"Her guilt."

Grigg shook his head and returned his gaze to the view of the solar cluster on his monitor. "No. I'm sorry. I was—"

"Feeling fucked up and weird about your feelings toward me?"

9

onrav

"Fuck, Rav. Why do you do that?" Grigg's mouth thinned into a fine line and he refused to look at me. I'd never seen Grigg look embarrassed, not in all the years I'd known him.

I reached out and put my hand on his shoulder, hard. I squeezed when he tried to shrug me off. This was something we had to talk about. If our mating with Amanda was going to work, we needed to work this out. "Look, I don't mind. I don't want to fuck you, Grigg, but if allowing you to be a bossy asshole in bed gets Amanda that hot and bothered every time we're together, I am yours to command. She was so fucking wet, so desperate for us, I couldn't think. She loved it."

"I know."

"And the rest of it?"

He looked at me now, and I knew he'd already buried the rest of his emotions so deep I'd have to force them back to the surface. "Look, I felt it all, Grigg. These fucking collars don't let us hide anything. You were feeling territorial, and it wasn't just about Amanda."

"I'm sorry. I don't know where it came from." Grigg looked so lost, so out of his element that I believed him. Which was just fucking sad, and further testament to how badly his unfeeling asshole of a father had fucked him up.

"It's normal, Grigg. It's called love. Concern. Affection. You're my cousin, and I love you. I'd die for you, kill to protect you. It's perfectly normal that you'd feel the same. That just makes us a family. And all those feelings now extend to our mate. I feel it, too."

"I've never felt any of that before."

"The fucking collars," I muttered. "I know. But now *you* know."

"Know what?"

"What family is supposed to feel like."

Grigg rubbed his chest and I felt the pang of emotion that was ripping him to shreds. He had no idea what to do with all of the sentiment, so I helped him out with a bit of distraction. "So, back to our mate. I think we might have a problem."

"The guilt?"

"Yes. She's hiding something. Those collars sense everything, even that."

Grigg frowned, his mind now focused on solving a real problem, something he could deal with so much more efficiently than his unfamiliar emotions. "What do you suspect?"

I hated to say it, but when I'd found out our mate was coming from a new member of the Interstellar Coalition, I'd done some research. "I looked up her planet, read every report about Earth."

"And?"

"Her people are primitive, still fighting wars over resources and land. In many parts of her world, women are still denied basic rights and education. They are treated as slaves without honor or power in their own right. They allow their poor to starve and die in the streets. They kill over skin color and religious beliefs. They're barbaric."

"She's no longer an Earthling. She's a citizen of Prillon Prime. She belongs to us now."

"Yes, officially."

"But?"

"She had two men with her at the processing center. She said they were her family, lied to the Warden, but they were not related to her. Suspicious, the Warden reviewed the recording of their conversation."

"And who were they?"

"Spies. Apparently, Amanda is a spy for her government."

Grigg's eyes widened. "Amanda, a spy?"

I nodded.

"Yes. She's the first Bride. It makes sense to use the program to their advantage. I assume they sent her here to send information to Earth, to steal advanced technologies that the Coalition has denied them."

"I see." I could literally feel his mind working, calculating odds, formulating a plan. "And how do you know this? Is the information about our mate reliable?"

"Absolutely. I asked the primary Warden on Earth, Lady Egara, to dig into her past."

Grigg leaned forward. "I thought Earth just found out about the Coalition. And I know Commander Egara. What is his mate, a Prillon Lady, doing on Earth?"

The answer to that question was sad, indeed. "Both of Lady Egara's mates were lost in a Hive ambush a few years ago."

"Gods have mercy." Grigg frowned at that and I felt his sadness over the news. "No children?"

"No. And she refused another match. She was taken from Earth years before official contact was made with the planet. I don't know the details, but after her mates' deaths, she offered to serve on Earth as the leader of the Bride Processing program there. In any event, her loyalty is to the Coalition. I trust her information."

Grigg rose to pace and I watched, inclined to let him decide a course of action. I was trained to heal, not deal with subterfuge and battle. And I knew for a fact that the war for our bride's heart and loyalty had barely begun.

Arms across his chest, Grigg turned to me. "Do you wish to give her up? Ask for another mate?"

"No. She was matched to us. The testing was done. It was ninety-five percent accurate. There is no question from Warden Egara, or me, that she is the one for us. She's ours now, whether she realizes it or not. Whether her loyalties lie with her government or with us, her mates."

"Agreed." Grigg resumed pacing the small space. "This would explain Earth's eagerness to send their first group of warriors into Hive combat."

That was a surprise. "They are eager to send their soldiers?"

"Yes. Too eager. They didn't even want to allow their soldiers to complete the training protocols." He shook his head. "Which is stupid, and suicidal. Their general's report claims these men are something they call *Special Forces*, and will not require extensive training. They are Earth's elite warriors."

I smiled at Grigg's expression. Game on. "So, what are you going to do?"

"Let them come, and use our beautiful little mate to lead us to the traitors among them. Surely they would not just send one spy."

"And after?" The idea made me nervous. I knew Grigg would never harm a hair on our mate's head, but I wasn't so sure about the soldiers who would be coming from Earth.

"Kill the traitors and spank her ass a fiery red. She has been matched to us. Like you said, there is no question as to that, that she's ours. We're going to fuck her and fill her until she knows exactly who she belongs to, and it's not the tribal rulers on Earth. They can't fuck her and love her like we can."

"No. She might be their spy, but she belongs to us."

––––––

AMANDA

I STIRRED at the sound of an odd beep. It happened only once, so I ignored it, rolling over. Being used to sleeping in new places all the time because of work, I woke knowing exactly where I was. Space. It also helped that my pussy and ass were both quite sore and I could never forget what Grigg and Rav had done to me. The plug had been removed directly after Grigg fucked me, while I'd been wilted and sated, then I'd fallen asleep between them.

The beep came again. Lifting my head, I looked about the bedroom. I was alone, the bed cold on either side of me. I didn't get out of bed after my mates left earlier, especially not after Rav's kiss. The gentle touch had melted the anger out of me on the spot and I'd drifted back to sleep, been dead to the world since.

Beep!

Grabbing the sheet and wrapping it around me, I went out into the living room, noting for the first time the small table with three chairs, the oversized couch bolted to the floor, the stark walls and utilitarian emptiness of the plain brownish walls. The whole thing screamed bachelor pad, and I wondered what kind of decorations I might find to make it feel more like a home and less like a hospital room.

Regardless, the room was empty.

Beep!

It came from the door. It seemed to be a space doorbell. I

went over to it, but there wasn't a doorknob. Perhaps it was motion activated, for as soon as I was within three feet of it, it slid open.

A woman was there, smiling at me. Garbed in a similar uniform to the one Rav had worn the day before, while his shirt had been green, hers was a pale peach color. But she was not human. Her shoulder-length hair was pulled back in a braid, but that didn't hide the dark orange color of the strands. She towered over me in the entryway, almost a foot taller than I. Her eyes, while kind, were a golden color I was getting used to, her skin a dark gold similar to Grigg's. Her voice, however, sounded perfectly normal.

"You are the commander's mate? Lady Zakar?"

Her voice was soft, kind, yet she had the erect posture of a soldier, of a woman who did not cow to anyone.

Gripping the sheet snugly, I flushed, for I could only imagine what she thought of me. I felt like I was doing the walk of shame, but had nowhere to go.

"Yes," I replied. "I...um. I'm Amanda."

When two soldiers entered the hallway, the woman glanced at them as I shifted back behind the doorway, then returned her attention to me.

"I'm Lady Myntar, but you can call me Mara. Your mates sent me. May I come in?"

Hearing the soldiers' voices coming closer, I nodded and stepped back, not wanting them to see me like this, naked, used and wearing only a sheet.

She entered and the door slid closed behind her. I breathed a sigh of relief.

"As I said, your mates sent me as they could not be here when you woke."

That was considerate of them.

"I'm in charge of family integration and socialization and have mates of my own. One of them, my Drake, works with

Commander Zakar. You are a lucky woman to find such an exemplary mate and a highly respected second." She leaned forward and spoke in a hushed tone. "But don't let my own mates know I said that."

I smiled then, for she was quite nice and I hadn't realized I needed...someone. Someone who wasn't planning on stripping me down and fucking me. At least right now. I needed reassurance that being on a Prillon ship was about more than just being mated to two warriors. While I had enjoyed what they did to me the night before and my body ached for them—their seed still trickled from my pussy—I was more than just a mate. If I had to sit inside this small room and stare at the walls for days on end, I'd go stark, raving mad.

"I'm here to help you with clothes and food, to start. And if you need anything else, just let me know. I will help you find work you'll enjoy. Friends. Something to fill your days while your mates are busy. I think it must be quite different for you here than on Earth."

I had no idea yet exactly how it was different, but I tugged at the sheet. "Anything will be better than this sheet. Thank you. But I'd love to shower first."

She smiled then. "Of course."

Mara spent the next hour showing me how to use the bathing units—there was both a shower and a bathtub, although she told me they were for pleasure and not strictly necessary. She showed me the S-Gen, where the green lights scanned my body and created new clothes for me to wear. The living space was completely unlike those on Earth as there was no kitchen, no closets and I followed her around almost blindly, with a curiosity only seen in small children. Several compartments were hidden in the walls and I anticipated finding and opening them all just like a treasure hunt. I felt like an excited child being hand held and I was thankful for it. I told her so.

"You're welcome. I will take you to the cafeteria. After that, you should be set with everything. Oh!" She spun on her heel and faced me. "Your mating box. I understand it was not claimed in the medical unit."

"Mating box?"

She waved her hand through the air. "It's a box of supplies for new mates. We'll just go and retrieve one from the commissary. Would you like to see some of the ship before we eat?"

The idea of seeing more than just Grigg's quarters was appealing and I ignored the rumbling in my stomach. I was hungry, but I could wait. Not only would it slake my curiosity, but it would allow me to investigate and study the ship so I could report back to Earth.

"Yes, please."

Dressed now in a midnight-blue uniform of dark pants and matching tunic, I finger combed my hair and left it down in a wild tangle around my shoulders and eagerly followed Mara out into the hallway. There wasn't much to see, only a plain orange hallway. The walls changed from orange to green to blue as we progressed through the ship, Mara explaining as we went that orange or cream shades indicated we were in civilian or family areas, green was medical, blue engineering, red was command and battle stations. The ship was color-coded, as were the uniforms, with gray being general support staff, the color of the insignia on their chests indicating in which area of the ship they served. High-ranking officers, such as doctors and engineers wore uniforms that matched their ship's section. Which explained Rav's dark green uniform.

Warriors, like my Grigg, all wore an intriguing black and dark brown camo armor that Mara insisted was nearly indestructible, explaining, "The commander has tested it, often."

I didn't like the sound of that.

We passed several people who all nodded their heads

deferentially. At first I thought it was how they said hello, but it appeared they were only doing it for me, not Mara.

"Why are they nodding to me? They don't even know me."

"They know you are the commander's mate, our Lady Zakar. We have waited several years for your arrival."

I frowned as we turned a corner. "How do they know it's me?"

Mara pointed to my neck. "Your collar. Your clothing. Your alien appearance. The commander insisted you wear the Zakar family color. The color is different for each group of mates. See —" She pointed to her own neck. "My mate's family line, the Myntar warrior clan, is represented by dark orange."

"I'm honored, but confused. Why would anyone here be waiting for me?"

Mara stopped walking and turned to face me. "The commander's mate has great power and influence. In regards to civilian matters, your orders are to be followed by all on board, warriors and civilians alike. None but the commander himself may order you around, and all on board would die to protect you. You are like a princess now, or a queen. Our queen."

What the fuck? I couldn't keep the shock, or the nerves from my voice. "Why? What am I supposed to do? Why would a warrior follow my orders? Am I supposed to go into battle?"

"Oh, no, dear." She patted me on the sleeve, then dropped her hand. "No. Although, if you really wanted to, and could convince your mates to allow it, you could. No. I will help you find a job that suits you. As the highest-ranking Lady of the ship before your arrival, I have been in charge of the civilian side of life in space. The warriors are busy fighting and expect the non-combat personnel to handle the rest."

Holy shit. "Like what?"

"Adoptions, matings, maintenance, socialization, community, schooling—"

I held up my hand, interrupting, "So, they fight and we take care of everything else?"

"Exactly." She grinned. "And I would love to have your help, if you are interested."

"But, how do you know I won't make a horrible mess of things? I don't know anything about your ships, or your way of life. I didn't even know a space ship existed outside of movies until recently."

Mara's smile was fill of confidence, and I couldn't stop the warm glow her words elicited. "You are his match. Perfect for him, which means you must also be perfect for us. The protocols would not have mated our commander to a woman who could not handle him, or responsibilities of her own."

Stunned, I felt my mouth open and close, which made her laugh.

"My mate is Captain Myntar, the third-highest ranking officer in Battle Group Zakar. And since neither the commander nor Captain Trist was mated, I've been running things around here by myself. And between you and me, I could *really* use some help."

Excitement tingled up my spine at the prospect of having something meaningful to do. I should have been excited at the opportunities I would have to gather information in my new role, but, if I were honest with myself, it felt good to be productive. I loved the idea of contributing to something, building something, rather than destroying it.

"How long have you been a mate?" I asked.

"Five years. We have a son." Her face lit up. "Would you like to see him?"

"Oh, um...sure."

"Good, because I took him to his school—he's only three, so it's more for play—but I always like to peek at him and see him having fun."

We turned a few more corners, the wall color changing

again to a soft, sandy brown. Zara stopped in front of a door long enough for it to slide open, then I followed her in. We were in an entry area, an odd blue-skinned woman sat behind a desk. Her hair was as black as her eyes, but her features were stunning, cover-model gorgeous.

"Lady Myntar," the woman said.

"Hi, Nealy. This is Lady Zakar—"

The woman stood, nodded her head. "The commander's mate. Welcome."

I smiled at the young woman. "Thank you. And you can call me Amanda."

Mara was practically glowing. "I just wanted to take a peek at Lan. I won't disturb."

Nealy nodded and we approached one of the windows that offered a view into the adjacent rooms. There were various-aged children playing in each, adults with them and playing too, some helping with coloring or rolling a ball.

"There." Mara pointed to a little boy with the same golden coloring and rust-colored hair as his mother. He was busy stacking blocks with a little girl with flaxen hair, similar to my Rav's. The scene was straight out of any preschool back home.

"He's adorable."

Mara beamed, clearly enthralled by her child. "Yes. He is so strong. Already so protective. He punched another little one yesterday for pulling on little Aleandra's hair. His fathers were so proud."

Okay, so they encouraged fighting.

No, they encourage their little boys to protect the little girls. I couldn't say I disapproved.

We watched for a few minutes, enjoying the simple joy on their faces, their innocent delight in such basic things. I realized these children were just like little boys and girls on Earth. They were no different. One stole a toy from another, one had fallen asleep on a blanket with a book. Another sat in one of the teacher's laps, tears on his cheeks. She was waving a small glowing wand over a scraped knee.

I pointed. "What's that?"

"The ReGen wand?"

"The thing in the teacher's hand."

"Yes. It's a healing wand."

Within seconds, the boy's knee was completely healed, no sign of the scrape remained. His tears stopped and he was smiling.

"I've never seen one before," I commented.

"We should go before Lan sees me."

We left the little school and took to the corridors again.

"You'll find a ReGen wand in all of the community areas. In the work areas as well. They heal minor injuries, but if you're truly hurt, you can go to the medical stations, that's where they have the ReGen pods."

"It heals things quickly, too, like that boy's knee?"

"Yes. They're actually called Regeneration Submersion Units, but we call them pods."

Wow. I had visions of a coffin-style pod, straight out of a sci-fi movie. Lie down in the pod, wait a few minutes, completely healed? Earth could really use something like that.

And the ReGen wand? It was portable, easy, quick. It could change the face of medicine on Earth, but we didn't know about it. I had to remember to look for the one Mara had said would be in a community area. If all else failed, I would have to swallow the bitter distaste rising in my throat and steal the ReGen wand in the preschool. Surely, they would replace it immediately. They had to have thousands of the things.

I accompanied Mara to a large cafeteria-style dining area, which was mostly empty. She showed me how to order food from the S-Gen unit, told me I could also order food in my room, but that eating alone was frowned upon in Prillon society and the warriors and their mates would take it as a slight if I did not join them in the common areas, especially me, their commander's mate. *Their* Lady Zakar.

Great. Now I had princess duty complete with politics and public appearances? That was more than I'd bargained on. A lot more.

The food was strange, crisp noodles that tasted like a mixture of orange peel and peaches. A strange purple fruit that was shaped like an apple, but tasted like tart cherries, like the ones my grandmother used to use baking pies.

I did my best, I truly did, but my distaste must have shown on my face. Mara laughed at me. "You know, you can ask the commander to request our programmers include some dishes from Earth."

"I can?" Thank God. I could survive on this stuff, but it wasn't going to win any blue ribbons at a county fair. It would certainly help my waistline.

"Yes. Give him a list. Once he's signed off on it, we'll submit the list to the programming teams on Prillon Prime. They'll request the dishes from Earth, analyze the content and program them into the S-gen unit for you."

"Thank you! That would be wonderful." I wanted to hug her, I truly did.

"We must go now."

I nodded. She'd spent nearly the entire day showing me around the ship, introducing me to everyone we met. I was fine smiling and nodding and generally doing my best to be a people person, but even I had my limits, and they'd all been tested the last two days. I was ready for some peace and quiet. I needed time to think, to figure out what I was going to do.

I followed her out of the cafeteria, down a series of corridors until we arrived at an odd counter. Mara walked up to it, the woman behind it reminded me of a pharmacist at a drug store or even a ticket seller at a movie theater. I wasn't sure exactly what the woman's role might be.

"One ATB, please." Mara requested.

The Prillon woman glanced at me briefly, nodded, then went into a small room behind her to retrieve one. She handed it to Mara, who handed it to me.

"What is this? What's an ATB?" I took the box, about the size of a small shoebox, and tucked it under my arm.

"ATB stands for Anal Training Box. That's not the official name, that's just what we ladies like to call it."

10

 manda

"WHAT?" She did *not* just say what I thought she said.

Mara took off down the hallway, clearly expecting me to follow. "I must go to work, so I will return you to your family quarters. Doctor Zakar assured me one of them would return to you soon. I do not want them to be worried if they have already returned."

Neither had, in fact, come back. Alone, I opened the box, curious as to what was in it.

ATB. Anal—seriously?

Within was more than a dozen oddly shaped tools with bulbous ends, strange twisting middles, and open-ended tools that looked more like wrenches, or something that might be used to fix a car. Shaking my head, I ran my fingertip over the long, bumpy length of one extremely odd, silvery item that appeared to be glowing.

I had no idea what any of them were used for, and none

appeared to be anything used for the...um...anal area. I had to assume at least one of them would be something Robert might want, like the ReGen wand. The agency sought technology and here was an entire box full. No matter what its use, I was sure the agency's scientists could reverse engineer something useful from it. And the healing tool. I had to get my hands on one of those things, and figure out a way to transport it back home.

I rummaged around and found one item that looked unusual. Pulling it out, I fiddled with it, wondering what it was. It was a bar about six inches long with two circles at each end. Made of lightweight metal, it was fairly basic, looked like a double ended socket wrench. Weird.

Holding the strange item, I wandered through our quarters, fiddling with the ends, trying to figure out what, exactly, it might be used for. I was near the couch when I heard the door slide open, and Grigg call for me.

"Amanda. Have you returned?"

Panicked at being caught with the oddity, I bent quickly to hide it under the dark blue couch cushion.

"Mate!"

Just his deep voice had my heart thumping, my pussy aching. I spun about to look at him where he stood a few steps behind me, hands on his hips. I'd been caught with my hand under the cushions and my ass in the air. I knew my face flushed, and the heat in my face worsened as he raised one dark brow.

"I'm sorry to have left you alone. You look as if Mara has taken care of you."

He closed the distance between us and whispered, "I love the way the dark blue Zakar color clings to your round ass. Although I believe I like you even better in just a sheet."

I heated at his honeyed words, at the eagerness of his tone. Just hearing his voice, having him in the same room was arousing.

"What are you hiding?" he asked, nodding toward the couch.

I had no choice but to pull the object from beneath the thick cushion and hold it up.

"I don't know, actually," I replied, honestly. While hiding it might appear to be odd, I didn't have to lie about anything else. Standing, I pointed to the box. "We retrieved a mating box, but I haven't figured out how the items are used."

Grigg put his fingers on the edge of the box and slid it across the table, peered inside. "Yes, I am familiar with the box. But tell me, mate, why were you hiding that one item specifically?"

"I... I—" I used to be able to fake my way out of any situation. From Australia to Arizona, I could make things up on the fly. But now... "I don't know."

Grigg offered a noncommittal grunt in reply. "You are aware, mate, that the collars we share also allows us to recognize emotions. For example, you should have sensed that I was highly aroused when I came in. My need for you would most likely intensify any arousal you had of your own."

That made sense, for I'd instantly craved him when he returned. I still did, in fact.

"It also senses other emotions, like nervousness." He took the object from me, turning it over in his large hands. "Or lies."

I swallowed then. Damn technology. How the hell was I supposed to be a spy when my every thought and feeling was exposed?

"I really don't know what that is."

He reached into the box and pulled out a much smaller one. "I asked Mara to make sure you received your box. In our haste, we did not collect one from the medical station after your exam."

I flushed at the memory of that exam.

"What are all those things?" I asked.

He opened the lid, lifted a layer I had not yet explored and pulled out what I could easily tell was a butt plug.

I said nothing, my core heated, my pussy and ass clenched. Suddenly ATB made a whole lot more sense. Surely not everything in the box was—

He grinned. "All new mates are given a set for training. We cannot be fully bonded until Rav and I claim you together, fuck you together."

"Oh," I replied, thinking about being between the two of them, their cocks both filling me to the brink. Just like my dream. Damn my wanton body, but everything kept going back to that dream. Two men. Both of them fucking me, filling me, making me theirs.

"Apparently Mara felt we needed not only the basic box of plugs, but much more elaborate supplies."

I pointed to the metal bar object and frowned at it. "That is a sex toy?" I asked.

"A sex *toy*." Grigg nodded. "I like that term, for this is definitely a toy, one I am eager to play with."

Me? I had doubts about that, for it looked more like a two-headed wrench than a toy.

"You were trying to hide a sex toy in the couch. Tell me once more, why?"

Oh shit. I bit my lip, stared at it. "I...I don't know. It was stupid."

He took it from me, considering.

"Yes, you said that, and I told you that I know the words are a lie."

Yeah, that hadn't worked the first or the second time. Shit.

"You hid it because you didn't want me to use it on you?"

I nodded then, perhaps more fervently than necessary.

"But you don't know what it is. How can you say you won't like it?"

I shrugged because I had no answer.

"What if I told you that you'd like it? That I'd never use something on you that you wouldn't enjoy? Would you trust me to use it with you?"

His eyes were so dark, so serious, and yet his voice was soft and gentle. He was coaxing me, for I had a feeling he wanted to use that toy. On me. Right now.

"It won't hurt?" I asked, eyeing the odd gadget.

"It's a pleasurable pain." When I took a step back and looked skeptical, he added, "Trust me."

I licked my lips and looked at him. *Really* looked at him. Did I trust him?

"If you don't trust me yet, trust our match. Trust that I know what you like, what you want. What you *need*."

"I need that?" I pointed to the mystery toy.

"Let's find out. Take off your shirt."

I looked at the small metal object in his hands, then at Grigg. He stood patiently, calmly waiting for me to decide just how adventurous I was willing to be.

"You want me to take off my shirt."

"I want you naked and begging, but we'll start with the shirt."

Shit. Why did he have to say things like that? So damn hot. "What is that thing?" I asked, biting my lip.

He held it up. "This? It's for your nipples."

"My—" Said nipples tightened painfully at the idea of... whatever that thing did.

"Take off your shirt, Amanda."

"I... I—" I continued to balk, now truly a little nervous.

"The idea of me doing something to your nipples arouses you, doesn't it, mate?" Grigg took a step toward me. "I can see they're already hard, eager for whatever I'm going to do. I can feel your interest and desire for it through the collar. I bet if I explored your eager pussy with my fingers, I'd find you wet, too."

He took another step toward me, gently put the metal bar down on the table. It was ignored for now, his focus squarely on me. All that power, that size, the intensity, was aimed at me and I didn't have the power to resist it. To resist him. Waves of desire washed over me, made my pussy ache, made it swell, readying for his cock. My breasts plumped, my nipples were tight points. My skin heated.

"There's...there's something wrong with me." I'd never become so aroused so quickly before, and he wasn't even touching me. It was similar to when I'd put the collar on, my feelings overwhelming me.

"You're feeing my arousal, too. Our bonding has already begun, our seed, our bonding essence is already at work in your body. There are no secrets between mates. No false emotions or desires. That fact will help you overcome your fears."

He lifted a hand to my arm, but did not touch, slid it down through the air, but I felt the sizzle, the heat of that almost touch and I shivered.

"Bonding essence?"

"That fluid that drips from our cocks is for you. I rubbed it on your clit during the exam, to ease your fears. Then, when we fucked you, our seed coated your pussy, marked you. Filled you. The bonding chemicals in our seed enters your body, becomes essential. It's one way Prillon warriors bond with their mates."

"You guys drugged me with your semen?" I asked.

He shrugged and wasn't ashamed to admit it. "Drugged is not the right word. Your desire, your acceptance is just another sign that you belong to us. Right now, I have yet to touch you and you are close to coming. Am I wrong?"

I was breathing hard now, the room quite warm.

"No." I had to admit the truth, for it was obvious I was affected...somehow.

"Then trust me to make you feel good. Take. Off. Your. Shirt."

His voice dipped, had a sharp tone to it. He'd talked to me about my concerns, but now his patience was at an end. I could feel that, too.

Reaching for the hem, I lifted it up and over, tossing it to the floor. Grigg watched as I did so, kept his gaze squarely on my chest as it was revealed. The odd bra—like one from Earth with an underwire and cups, yet minus the full cup—exposed the top swells of my breasts. Like a demi-bra, only much more demi than anything I'd seen on Earth. If I breathed hard, I was sure my nipples would pop free.

With one finger, Grigg tested that theory, hooked the fabric along the plain edge of the white material and nudged it down. My nipple was revealed, all hard and taut. When he exposed my other nipple, I gasped, the cool air in the room hardened them farther.

"Gods, you're gorgeous," he exclaimed, exhaling a pent-up breath. I felt his desire ratchet farther, especially when he slid a knuckle down the full swell of one breast.

In that moment, I felt gorgeous, for his eyes, his expression, was one of eagerness, need and dark desire. His need was coiled tight, like a spring. Leaning forward, he took one tip into his mouth, sucked and laved it. My fingers went instantly to his hair, tangled in it and held on. After a minute, he switched to the other breast, did the same thing, then looked at both. They were bright pink and shiny from his ministrations.

"There, that's better."

I glanced at him with lust-filled eyes. I could only nod, for it was better, and yet infinitely worse because I was eager, so eager for more.

Without looking away, he grabbed the metal bar and held it in front of my breasts. With the press of a button, the width adjusted so that the circles were spaced apart the exact width of my nipples. Grigg pressed it gently against my breasts, shifting my soft flesh a little so that the nipple was placed in the center of the circle. He did this to one, then the other.

I looked down and watched, enthralled by the odd object. I only knew of nipple clamps that were like little clips, pinching the nipples. Sometimes decorative jewelry or chains dangled down. But this...this was different, a bar attached with what? Suction? A cinch? I wasn't sure how it worked.

He flicked his gaze to mine. "All right?" he asked.

It didn't hurt at all, the metal warm against my skin, so I nodded.

He pressed another button in the middle and a pale yellow light came on. At the same time, the aperture on the circles around my nipples narrowed until Grigg was able to take his hand away, the toy remaining on. The pressure wasn't too bad, but I did gasp. My already tender nipples were being squeezed ever so slightly.

The light changed color to a darker yellow.

"That's it," Grigg said, lifting his own shirt up and shucking it to the floor.

Oh my. His chest was massive, and rippling with muscles. His shoulders were broad, twice the width of my own and all that power tapered to a ripped abdomen and, I knew, a huge cock that I could see was already hard and ready to take me.

"That's it?" I repeated, looking down at myself. It didn't hurt, but it wasn't arousing either. "It's not much of a toy," I replied, oddly disappointed.

"Well, I'm not fucking you yet," he countered.

I frowned at him as he stripped down completely. His armor fell to the floor and he placed something on a small stand between the chair and the bed. I didn't see what he placed there, for his cock was erect and bobbing between us and captured my complete attention.

"The toy—as you call it—senses your arousal, senses what

you need to assist in achieving orgasm and will tighten the pressure on your nipples accordingly."

I looked at the innocuous object again. "Are you serious?"

He grinned and came over to me, worked the remainder of my clothes off so I was naked. He'd even carefully removed my bra.

"Gods, look at you. Did men on Earth tell you how spectacular you are?"

I opened my mouth, thinking back to the men I'd been with in the past. None of their faces came to mind, for I'd felt nothing like I did with Grigg and Rav.

He held up a hand. "Never mind. Do not answer that. Do not think of other men when I touch you, or I shall have to spank your perfect ass and fill you with my cock until you remember that you belong to me."

I wanted to laugh, but I sensed that he wasn't completely joking.

"You're ours, Amanda. Mates. You feel it, you know it."

I flushed, for I felt the truth of his words through the collar, the burst of arousal he felt when he looked at me. The circles about my nipples tightened slightly and I gasped. The color on the bar shifted to orange.

He winked at me, knowing the clamps had tightened.

"I like watching your face when the toy starts playing with your hard nipples. I want to watch your face when you come all over my cock."

I moaned then, for the words were just what I wanted to hear.

He sat down in a chair, legs spread wide, crooking his finger.

I moved toward him, the odd feel of the bar between my breasts more distracting since the slight increase in the tightness.

With one hand hooked about my waist, he pulled me to

him so I straddled his hips, my breasts directly in line with his face. With the lightest of touches, Grigg licked my breast all around the outside of the metal circle, first one, then the other. The circle tightened.

My fingers tangled in his hair, wanting to keep his mouth directly over me. I writhed on his lap, shifting and rubbing his cock against my belly. I could feel his pre-cum seep from him and coat both our skins. The heat of it, the bonding essence, he called it, warmed me, spread through me like a drug. It *was* a drug, for I craved it. Needed it. Just the little stream that was coming from him was not enough. I wanted all of him, his cock buried deep and his seed coating my pussy.

"What about...what about Rav?"

I was not used to having two men. Was there a protocol regarding being with one of them without the other? Did one get jealous of the other?

"He is working. You are here, in need of a sex toy demonstration and a good fucking. We do not need to take you together all the time. You will find us insatiable, so be prepared to have your men on you morning, noon and night."

With his nose, he nudged the bar between my breasts. It elicited a gasp from me and a tug on his hair.

"Let's see how wet you are, how ready you are for my cock."

He pushed me away from him, his grip tight on my hips as he scooted my ass to his knees, holding my thighs over his as he spread his legs, forcing my pussy to open in the space between us, easy for him to see and touch. I placed my hands on his shoulders for balance. While I knew he would not let me fall, I needed some kind of anchor.

"Don't move." The two words barely registered before his hand left my right hip to cup my wet heat. I knew I was wet, for the air cooled my sensitive flesh where my juices coated the folds of my core.

He explored me with two fingers, holding my gaze trapped

with his own. I stared into his dark eyes as his fingers pushed slowly, so very slowly to fill me. His eyes filled with lust, need, desire and the look drove my arousal as much, or more than the bonding essence in his seed. No man had ever looked at me like he did, like he'd die if he didn't fuck me. Like I was the most beautiful woman in the world. His desire was addictive, it made me feel powerful despite the fact that I was his to command, his to control. And that dichotomy confused me.

I blinked.

"No, Amanda. You will not look away." Grigg fucked me with his fingers in a slow, sensual glide that wound me higher but would never give me the release I craved.

"I can't—you are too—" Two blunt fingertips touched me deep inside, stroking the entrance to my womb and my legs tensed as I jerked at the sensation. God, he was so fucking deep.

"Too what?" he growled.

I shook my head, unwilling or unable to answer. I wasn't sure which, my mind a scramble as the nipple toy suddenly turned a dark red, sending a small jolt of electric shock through the sensitive tips as it tightened farther, just enough to make me moan, a tickle of electricity.

Grigg sighed and removed one hand from my wet core and the other from my hip. I missed his touch instantly, suddenly feeling cold and empty, too alone. I longed for our physical connection, his touch a balm to my senses. I was free to stand, to get off his lap and walk away from whatever game we were playing. But I didn't. I stayed, right where I was, open and panting, scared to death of how much I wanted to please him. I wanted more. I wanted whatever he would give me.

When had I gone from brilliant, independent spy to needy, clingy woman? And why with him? Rav excited me, and I felt safe with him, desired and pleasured, but something about Grigg made me lose my freaking sanity. With Grigg, I lost myself, and that scared me more than anything ever had, more than being shot at during a high-speed chase, more than death itself.

The match is 95%...perfect for you in every way. Warden Egara's words came back to haunt me. That was the only explanation. The matching protocol must work, just as promised. Which meant Grigg must truly be mine. If that was true, he had to be honorable, loyal, honest. If he weren't, I wouldn't want him, wouldn't be attracted to him. Character mattered to me. Therefore, Grigg wouldn't be the kind of man to take advantage of an entire planet of people as Robert had insinuated. He just wouldn't. Was the CIA wrong? Were we just too new to the Coalition to understand or was I drugged by lust and blinded to the truth?

"You lied to me, Amanda."

"What?" Between my wet pussy, pinched nipples, thundering heart and my panicked mind, I couldn't process what he was talking about.

"You lied to me about the sex toys. About a lot of things, I'm afraid."

Nervous now, I tried to close my legs, but his hands came down on top of my things like clamps. "I don't know what you're talking about."

That sigh, the disappointment I felt coming from him through my collar made my heart actually ache.

"What were you doing with the box?"

"Nothing. Just looking." What could I say? *Oh, well, Grigg, I was trying to figure out how to send butt plugs and electronic nipple clamps back to Earth for the CIA?* That was beyond ridiculous, as I realized my actions truly were. Was I so desperate to follow orders that I'd send something from the Anal Training Box for them to dissect and analyze? That was stupid. And I wasn't a stupid woman. I rarely lied to myself, but it appeared I'd been doing a lot of that since my arrival here. Lying to myself and to my mates.

I remained silent until, moving so quickly I had no time to protest, I found myself bent over Grigg's knees, my ass in the air and his hand on my back, holding me in place. He was careful with the bar across my chest.

"You lied to me, again."

"No." I shook my head as I stared, wide eyed, at the floor.

His hand landed on my ass with a sharp sting and I gasped. "What do you think you're doing?"

"I'm spanking you. I told you, mate, that you would be punished for lying to your mates." His hand landed again, on the opposite cheek, and for some bizarre reason, the left was more sensitive than the right. My back arched and I cried out at the pleasure pain as heat built under my skin, spread to my thighs, my stomach, my clit. The nipple clamp tightened farther.

Smack!

Smack!

Grigg grunted, his rough hand kneading my bottom where he'd just spanked me, his voice rough, "Your ass is perfect, Amanda, so round. So lush. It wiggles so nicely when I spank you. I love the way it bounces when I fuck you."

When his next slap landed on my ass, I was even wetter than I'd been before, the sting spreading faster this time, right to my pinched nipples.

Smack!

Smack!

Smack!

I squirmed as the nipple clamps squeezed and released, pulsing over the sensitive tips, tickling them with electricity with every release, releasing with every sharp snap of Grigg's hand on my ass. The left. Right. Over and over he spanked me until I couldn't take any more, my body out of control and wild.

The hand on my back held me down, and I realized I had nowhere to go, no option but to submit as fire raced through my bloodstream and wet welcome coated my thighs. I cried out, not in upset or pain over the spanking, but with pleasure. Incredible, perfect, painful pleasure. God, this was so messed up, and I didn't care.

I was so fucking hot I was about to orgasm, and I didn't fucking care.

My mind went blissfully, utterly blank.

My body slumped in submission, eager for the next sharp sting of his spanking, of his dominance, eager for the final sensual bite of pain that would make me come.

11

 manda

THE SHARP PLEASURE of his hand on my ass never came and I whimpered a protest.

Pushing against the floor, I tried to lift myself from Grigg's lap.

"Hold still. I'm not finished with you."

I froze instantly, completely at his mercy, the commanding tone of his voice made my pussy tighten around frustrating emptiness. I wanted his cock. Now.

He reached for the object on the small table, the one I'd ignored earlier, and I realized it was one of the butt plugs from the box.

I dropped my head, unwilling to protest, because the truth was, I wanted it in my ass as he fucked me, and he would fuck me, eventually. The lust coming off him through the collar made me heady. I wanted the sensation of being completely full, stretched, claimed just as I'd enjoyed last night.

He made quick work of spreading my ass cheeks and working the lubricant into my body with one hard, thick finger. I breathed through his attentions. The plug, when it came, was bigger, wider and I knew he'd chosen one of the plugs with a bulbous head, one with a flat end that would hold the plug in place but allow it to move a bit within me as he fucked me with his cock.

The very idea made me whimper and I gripped his lower leg with one hand.

"That's right, mate. You're mine. Your pussy is mine. Your ass is mine."

His words made me squirm, and push back onto the object stretching me open. Grigg worked the plug into me slowly, carefully until my muscles gave way and it slid inside, deep inside, my body closing around it once more until the much thinner end rested against my ass, holding it in place. I groaned at how filled I was. Already I could feel the pressure increase inside my pussy and wondered how I could withstand the thick length of his cock filling me, too.

Would my body ache as he fucked me? And why did the idea of a little more pain mixed with my pleasure make me desperate to find out?

"Fuck me, Grigg. Please." I was so far past the embarrassment of begging.

My mate's answer was to spank my bottom again, the butt plug making the force of his palm transfer to my pussy, too. A cry escaped my lips.

"What were you doing with the box, Amanda?"

Damn it! Back to this? My frustration climbed to the breaking point and I felt tears gather in my eyes. "Nothing, okay? I was being stupid." I meant every word, and Grigg must have felt my truth through his collar, for the spanking stopped and I was lifted, carried to the wall near the far side of the bed.

Grigg set me down on my feet facing the wall and I reached

around to rub the soreness from my bare bottom. But Grigg had other ideas, grabbing my wrists, and as I looked over my shoulder at him, his eyes were almost black with intensity. "No. Your pain is mine. Your pleasure is mine."

God, he was an animal, so carnal and primitive and I loved it.

He slowly shook his head. "You do not touch yourself."

Right. I'd forgotten that one. So what was I supposed to do, let my butt burn?

He didn't leave me to wonder. He opened a small compartment in the wall to reveal a stationary set of cuffs attached to metal anchors just above shoulder height. In seconds, my wrists were bound by the alien version of cuffs. He pulled my hips backwards, a hand on my back so I bent at the hips, my arms stretched out above my head, the cuffs holding my wrists to the wall. The toy attached to my nipples hung low, tightened, released and clung, hanging on with a strange suction I'd not felt before.

I was just recovering from that when Grigg opened another storage space beneath the bed and removed a large bar and another set of cuffs, these for my ankles. I didn't fight him as he shoved my feet wide and strapped me in, the spreader bar would prevent me from closing my legs, from denying him anything he wanted.

———

GRIGG

MY MATE'S bare bottom was pink from her punishment, the butt plug firmly in place, increasing her pleasure, readying her body for the claiming, for Rav and me to fill her with both of our cocks. Her ankles cuffed and spread wide for my pleasure. I had bent her over, her ass in the air, her heavy breasts swinging beneath her, her long, elegant arms reaching the wall where another set of cuffs held her in place. Her exotic black hair rested against her paler skin, a frame for her beauty.

Our collars kept me in tune to her every desire, every reaction. I was pushing her, but I would know the second she was afraid, the second I took her beyond what she could handle. But her emotions were a confusing storm of lust and shame, frustration and desire, longing and guilt. No fear. My little human spy was cracking open, losing herself to me, but it wasn't enough. She still fought for control, and me? I wanted everything.

She was mine. All mine. Every beautiful, soft, wet, perfect fucking inch of her.

"Mine." I growled the word as I stepped forward, nudged the entrance of her pussy with my cock. The word sent a thrill through her, so I pushed deep in one slow, relentless stroke and tugged her hair, pulling her head up, angling it so she looked back over her shoulder, into my eyes as I repeated it. "Mine. Fucking mine."

Her pussy clamped down on me like a fist and I groaned with satisfaction at her response. She was so wet, so fucking hot. Her inner walls instantly rippled and clenched down on my cock.

I kept one hand in her hair, kept her eyes on mine as I shifted my stance, going deeper, lifting her feet off the floor with every thrust of my hard cock. I considered reaching beneath her to stroke her clit, but fucked her harder instead, barely able to withstand the added pressure of the plug. She was tight without it, with it?

Gods. So tight. So wet. So hot.

I slapped her ass just hard enough to offer her a slight sting of sensation on her already sore bottom, just hard enough to remind her that I was in control, that she was mine to do with as I pleased. My reward flooded our connection as she groaned, tilting her hips to take me deeper. Her juices flooded over my cock.

Desperation clouded her mind, the need to come filling her up and spilling over to me through our link.

One touch on her clit, one, and I knew she would shatter in my arms. But I didn't do that. Not this time. This time I wanted my seed to explode inside her, the bonding essence to saturate her senses, force her to come, over and over.

The thought of my seed inside her was all it took. My balls tightened, my cum shot forth and I emptied into her, roaring my release.

She held perfectly still, as if frozen solid or in shock as my seed filled her, as my claim grew stronger.

I felt her release rise within her like an ion blast shot into space, but she denied herself, held back. For me.

"Please." She waited, the one word a whimper of need.

I hadn't given her permission to let go.

In that moment, I was lost. I'd admired her, thought her beautiful, intelligent, brave. But this one act turned all those emotions to something so blinding and humbling, I knew I'd never felt it before. Love. It had to be love.

I draped my chest over her back and kissed her cheek softly, her face still turned to me, her hair still captured in my solid fist. One kiss, and I set her free.

"Come for me, love. Come now. I've got you."

Her body exploded and I covered her, wrapped my arm around her waist to hold her tight, grounded her as she broke into a million pieces in my arms. When one wave of release ended, all I needed to do was shift my hips and she shattered again. Twice. Three times.

My cock hardened inside her, ready to fuck her again. I did, softly this time, barely moving as the swollen walls of her pussy held me tight, milking me with such intense pleasure I did not want to pull free of her wet heat. Gods, she was perfect.

Releasing my hold on her hair, I moved my hands to cup her breasts, removing the nipple toy so I could play there myself, gently pulling and tugging, cupping and caressing as her ass squirmed and wiggled under my hips, her back so soft and long, elegant and curved under my chest.

She moved too much and I bit her shoulder to hold her in place, some long-buried animalistic instinct rising to cloud my mind as I emptied my seed into her pussy a second time.

Her next release was hard and fast and I did not want her to hold back. I knew she could not fight the bonding power of my seed, for it was too strong, too intense. She had no choice but to come. Her cries echoed through our bedchamber like the sweetest fucking music I'd ever heard and I knew I would never get enough of her. Never give her up.

When our breathing slowed I released her from her bonds and carefully removed the plug from her ass. The moment I was done, I pulled her into my arms and settled us on the bed for much needed recovery.

She curled against me like a contented pet and I stroked her sweaty back, her cheek, every bit of skin I could reach and marveled at the depth of my devotion. I knew my feelings would come to her through the collar, and I welcomed the bond. And yet, I had not forgotten the fact that my little mate was most definitely a spy for her world, sent here to infiltrate and betray me.

But I no longer cared. She'd been tested and matched. While there were ulterior motives perhaps, to her transport, there was no denying our connection. She was mine, I simply needed to work to gain her loyalty, her trust. The rest would fall away. I wanted her love, but I was a realistic man. That would take time I may not have. The combat units from her world were scheduled to arrive in two days. For the first time, I regretted my decision to allow them to transport so soon for I had no doubt there would be additional spies among Earth's soldiers. I was running out of time to win my mate, for there was no doubt they would attempt to sway her to their way of thinking. They would push her to work for Earth's best interest, not hers.

Her best interest? To be with her mates, the two males in the entire universe that were perfect for her.

I covered us with the soft blue blanket and contentment filled me as her arm snaked across my chest, her leg entwined with mine. Her mind was blank, empty. Happy. The feeling was addicting, and I knew I would destroy worlds to keep her right here, in my arms. Even as I entertained that thought, I knew I was about to ruin the moment.

"Amanda."

"Hmm?"

"I think we need to talk."

Her body tensed and I cursed myself a fool, but there was no getting around this. I had to know the truth. I *needed* her to trust me enough to tell me the truth. If what we just shared didn't show the connection and trust that could be between us, I wasn't sure what would.

"Okay. What do you want to talk about?" She shoved against my chest and I let her go, watched as she sat up and scooted to the head of the bed, pulling the blanket up to completely cover herself. I hated myself a little bit in that moment. Why couldn't I just enjoy the moment, the feel of her so soft and content in my arms? Even for five damn minutes?

Because I was a commander, responsible for thousands of soldiers, and billions of lives on the worlds we protected in this sector of space. Because I wanted the truth from her, to know that while the connection we shared while fucking was real, if it was still secondary to her main goal, to spy for her planet, to betray the Coalition and me.

Hell, I *wanted* her only goal to be to formally mate with me and Rav, to accept our claim, to stay forever.

Until she made her choice, I couldn't ignore the threat she presented.

"What is it, Grigg? I can feel your mind working."

"Rav contacted Warden Egara on Earth."

"He did? Why?" Anxiety spiked through her, and I knew Rav had been right.

Moving to sit beside her, I leaned my back against the wall but did not cover myself. I was a warrior, not a maiden. And if my cock was semi-hard for her again already, if it was still sticky with her arousal and my seed, then perhaps that would help me convince her that she mattered to me, that I cared for her more than I would have liked under the circumstances.

"He was curious about you, about where you came from, how you were chosen to be the first bride from your world."

She nibbled at her bottom lip and clenched the sheet tightly to her breasts, the knuckles turning white. "I'm not that interesting."

"On the contrary, I think an operative with a government agency assigned to infiltrate and spy on an alien battleship is incredibly interesting."

She froze, her dark eyes hidden as she blinked slowly, shock and relief bombarding me through the collar in equal measure. "What?"

"You heard me, mate."

She shook her head. "I don't know what you're talking about."

I rolled my shoulders. "I see you desire another spanking."

"No!" Her denial was sharp and immediate.

"Lies, Amanda. No more lies. What have you sent home to your precious agency?"

Her shoulders shuddered and I wanted to pump my fist

with victory as I felt her make the decision to talk to me. "Nothing."

"Why are you here?"

"Look, this whole Interstellar Coalition thing is new to us. We've never seen any evidence of the supposed Hive attack on Earth. Hell, we've never seen any evidence of the Hive's existence at all. You come to Earth and demand women and soldiers for *protection*." She lifted her hands, the first two fingers of each making a strange curling motion as she said the word. "It's all just a bit far-fetched and convenient for the Coalition forces. It's like a mafia shakedown for protection money."

I had no idea what half of her words referred to, but I'd caught the meaning behind her words. Earth did not believe us. "The Hive is very real, Amanda. I've been fighting them almost all my life."

She drew her knees up toward her chin and rested her bent arms atop them, her cheek resting on top as she turned her head to study me. "So you say, Grigg. But if the threat were real, why not give Earth weapons to defend itself? At the very least, share some of the healing technology I've seen here. The ReGen technology alone could save millions of lives."

Amanda's dark eyes were so serious, so contemplative, and I realized I enjoyed this side of her as much as I enjoyed the wild seductress who submitted to my sexual needs so beautifully. This was the leader I needed for my people, the true Lady Zakar I had begun to worry she might never be.

My hand shook as I lifted my fingers to stroke the delicate arch of her cheekbone, trace the fine line of her face. She did not pull away or deny me, simply watched me with the quiet intelligence I had begun to both expect and admire.

"Our Regeneration technology could save millions of lives, love, but it could be used to murder millions more. That is why we do not think it wise to share with the leaders of your world. They squabble over land and religion, fighting wars and killing tens of thousands while they already possess the technology to feed the hungry, heal their sick, care for all the citizens of Earth. They do not respect each other equally, do not educate their people, do not honor or protect their women. We would be fools to give such a powerful weapon to such primitive minds."

I watched her as she considered my words, weighed them for truth and accepted what I said. I did not lie, and our collars would transmit my sincerity to her as clearly as it sent her doubts back to me.

"What about the Hive?"

My thumb found her bottom lip and stayed, teasing the plump softness until she opened, letting me in just enough to nip at me with her teeth. "I do not want you anywhere near those evil bastards. But if you require proof, I will take you to the command deck with me in the morning. Our warriors are scheduled to destroy one of their Integration Units. I will show you what you want to see, Amanda, but you will not find what you seek."

"And what is that?"

"Confirmation of Earth's hope that the threat was fabricated. The Hive are dangerous and terrifying. Our warriors prefer death to capture. They consume all life they encounter with a ruthlessness that can only be created by the mind of a machine. You are suspicious now, love. But tomorrow you will be terrified."

She lifted her chin, my finger falling away. "At least I'll know the truth."

I shook my head and pulled her back into my arms, where she belonged. "No. You already know the truth. You already know what I tell you is accurate. The world you came from, those people you worked for—who think you still work for them—are no longer yours. You are Prillon now. You are a warrior bride of Prillon Prime, the Lady Zakar. I am telling you the truth. *We* are the truth. *You* are living the truth here, now, with us. You just don't want to accept it."

She didn't respond, for what could she say? She couldn't debate further, for her data was one sided. Tomorrow, when I took her to the command deck, when she had all the information she needed to make a qualified judgment, then we could discuss further.

Amanda drifted to sleep in my arms and I stared at the ceiling until Rav returned from working his shift. He took one look at us, the forgotten toys still laying on the floor, and chuckled. "You wear her out?"

"She told me the truth," I replied, my voice dipped low as not to wake her.

That got Rav's attention. "She admitted to being a spy?"

"Yes. I'm taking her to the command deck in the morning so she can watch the battle wings hit their closest Integration Unit."

Rav grimaced and shucked his clothes. "That'll turn her stomach. We lost an entire wing last week."

I felt Rav's anger through the collar and Amanda stirred. Perhaps she sensed it, too, even in sleep.

"I know. But she demands the truth, our human mate. And I promised to give it to her. The sooner she can see that, the sooner she will be ours. Completely."

Naked now, Rav crawled into bed behind Amanda and traced the curve of her hip with one hand, his exhaustion weighing heavily upon me through our link as he stilled and closed his eyes. "She just thinks she wants to know. It will terrify her, Grigg. It's too much. We could lose her."

"We'll lose her if we don't let her see the truth for herself."

Rav relented, for we both knew just how stubborn our beautiful mate could be. "I hope you know what you're doing, Grigg."

"As do I."

manda

THE COMMAND DECK of the *Battleship Zakar* was not what I expected it to be. I'd seen *Star Trek* more than once and I envisioned a bunch of chairs facing a view screen with the commander at the center sitting upon his throne like a king.

What a joke.

The room was round with a central aisle for walking and multiple viewing screens that descended from the ceiling at the center. Additional screens lined the upper third of the exterior walls as well. The space was nearly the size of a small café and much more active than I had imagined. The screens displayed planets and internal ship systems, communications and flight plans, schematics and reports that I didn't understand and had no way of comprehending. The objects chosen to be on display were seemingly controlled by more than one of Grigg's officers stationed around the outer rim of the room. Nearly thirty officers of varying ranks manned the workstations or hurried about. Communication was precise and orderly and the warriors all worked like a fine-tuned machine.

Some wore the black armor of battle-hardened warriors, some blue for engineering and red for weapons. There were three warriors wearing white. I didn't know what they did, and I didn't want to interrupt to ask. The air hummed with tension and that energy flowed through my mate and into me as he prepared to watch his warriors go into battle.

The preschool several floors below was a complete opposite of this. That, was life. This...this was life *and* death.

This wasn't their first battle, but it was mine. My palms were sweaty and I wiped them on the soft fabric of my blue tunic as I followed Grigg around the room like a puppy, listening to everything that was said, watching and absorbing everything I could. Those who looked away from their displays nodded to me deferentially, but I felt as if the respect was a distraction. *I* felt like a distraction for them, for Grigg. But he wanted me to see. Needed me to do so.

I saw weapons displays, ship tracking systems, navigation arrays that would make the astrophysicists and engineers at NASA drool. It was all here, and Grigg hid nothing from me. Nothing.

"Commander, the Eighth Battle Wing is in position. As is the transport shuttle."

Grigg nodded. He'd told me the battle wings would take out any resistance as the shuttle landed to retrieve any captives the Hive might have taken. They were protection, the muscle for the helpless shuttle. When the captives were freed, the fighters would destroy the small Hive outpost. My mate walked to the only empty seat in the room. Positioned between the red of weapons' controls and the blue of engineering, he motioned for me to sit beside him and I did.

"The Fourth?" he asked.

"Ready, Sir."

"Get Captain Wyle on comms."

"Yes, Sir." A few seconds later the screen directly before me filled with the face of a golden-eyed Prillon Warrior, his face slightly obscured by a pilot's helmet.

"Commander?"

Grigg stood and paced. "Wyle, what's your status?"

The captain's eyes darted around, checking data and systems we could not see. "We're a go, Commander. I'm only reading three scout ships and no soldiers. Should be an easy clean-up, Sir."

Grigg nodded. "All right, Captain. It's your op. We'll be monitoring from here. It's a go."

"Understood." The captain's face disappeared from the screen, but Grigg's agitated pacing increased as he muttered under his breath.

"Something doesn't feel right. It's too fucking easy."

A massive warrior with gold bands around his wrists, an Atlan Warlord I remembered, turned to Grigg from his station at the weapons display. "You want me to call them back?"

Grigg shook his head. "No, it's Captain Wyle's call now."

"Everything checks out, Sir. The scout patrols didn't pick up any additional Hive presence on the moon. Just the Integration Units." The giant had dark brown hair, his skin more human than anyone else's I'd seen so far on board the ship. He wore black armor, not red, and by the tight lines of tension around his eyes and mouth I knew he was as unhappy to be trapped in here for this operation as Grigg.

"I know." Grigg's eyes darted to me and I was well aware I was part of the reason for his anxiety, his nervous tension. I felt it through the collar easily enough, but it was just in the air too. The pressure, the intensity of what was about to unfold. I wanted to reach out and assure him that I was fine. I'd been in much more frightening situations than this. I was no delicate wallflower to be sheltered and protected. I wanted to know what was going on out there. I needed to know.

"It's begun." A young warrior in white spoke and everyone turned frantically to their monitors. In seconds multiple screens were ablaze with shots firing, explosions and the muted sounds of battle filled the room. It was like watching space fighters with live-action cameras attached to their cockpits. A dozen different screens tracked the fighter pilots as they fought the Hive ships. Explosions were muted on our end, as were their rapid-fire communications, the pilots' voices a constant stream of chatter I struggled to break into comprehensible order.

"Two more on your tail."

"Fire! Fire! Fire! I've got three coming from behind the moon."

"I see them."

"Where did they come from? Fuck. I can't see them."

"Wyle, I'm hit!"

"Eject, Brax! Now!"

Grigg growled and one of the men in white moved frantically at his station, communicating with someone I couldn't see. Whatever he was doing must have been expected because Grigg turned to him immediately.

"The shuttle?"

"No go. They're already on the surface. Closest pickup is three minutes away."

"Fuck. That's not fast enough." Grigg's jaw tightened and I knew he believed the warrior to be doomed.

True to Grigg's prediction, I watched a bright flare of yellow head toward the pilot floating in space like a rolling target. I stopped breathing as the orb engulfed him, his screams of agony filling the small room as the warriors in the ships around him spurred to action, taking out the Hive ship that had fired the shot.

"Kill that fucker!"

"Brax! Damn it!"

"Move Fourth, we've got more coming from the surface."

"Fuck. How many? I don't see anything."

"I don't see—wait. Fuck. Ten. No, twelve. Can someone fucking confirm twelve?"

"Another three here. Abort. There's too many." I recognized Captain Wyle's voice. "Shuttle crew, get out of there. Now. All fighters into defense formation. Let's get the fuck out of here. Commander Zakar? This is Wyle."

"I'm here."

"We're coming in hot. Nothing on our system scans, but visual count at fifteen fighters and they are in pursuit."

"Understood. Hang on. We're coming."

"Fucking hurry up, Commander, or we're all dead."

Grigg turned to one of the warriors in red. "Scramble the Seventh and the Ninth. Now. All pilots. I want them gone in sixty seconds."

The warrior didn't answer, just turned to his station and spoke to someone as bright lights and warning dings sounded from his workstation.

The dipping and zooming, the high-speed motion on the screens made me sway. I was grateful to have the chair to hold on to as motion sickness loomed. Determined not to look away I tried to track and understand the images moving at speeds that made me dizzy. I felt helpless, weak, useless. I could only imagine what Grigg felt like, his men out there under his command, under fire. Dying.

All around us battle chatter sounded as the pilots spoke to one another, fending off the pursuit. A small celebration sounded as the reinforcements arrived and the Hive fighters broke off their chase, turning around to flee in the opposite direction, back to wherever the hell they'd come from.

Captain Wyle's voice came through loud and clear. "They're running, Sir. Do you want us to pursue?"

"Negative. What I want you to do is find out how we were surprised by an entire fucking squadron of Hive scout ships."

"Copy that, Sir."

The mood in the room settled to a busy hum, one of recovery after an explosion and I leaned back in the chair, my pulse pounding and my mind racing as the pilots reported in. The battle had been real, the poor pilot, Brax, dead. But my curiosity remained unsatisfied. I wanted to see the face of the enemy, I wanted to *know* what they were.

I was so tense I felt like I was going to throw up in my mouth. Some of the tension was mine, but no small part came from Grigg, the energy and rage flowing through him in a tidal wave of raw hatred so intense I could barely comprehend it. Grigg *hated* the Hive with a vehemence that was a sucker punch to my gut. And I'd doubted this war. I'd doubted *him*.

But on the surface my mate's face was stone cold, calm as granite, and I marveled at the façade, the iron control required to govern the storm of power I felt brewing beneath his skin. My admiration for him grew as he anchored the crew with his level voice and confident stride. His power kept chaos at bay, his will alone all that stood between life and death for so many, both on the ship with us and out there fighting for their lives in space.

The warrior in white turned to Grigg. "The shuttle reports two survivors from the Hive base were brought on board, Sir."

Grigg's shoulders tightened and the pain that flooded me through our bond was old and deep, like a broken bone that refused to heal. On the surface? Nothing showed, not even a twitch of his eyelid nor the smallest frown. I wanted to soothe him, hug him, take some of the pain away. "Alert medical."

"Yes, Sir."

Grigg turned to me then and held out his hand. His jaw was

tense. Every line of his body was tense. "You want to see the face of our enemy, understand them?"

"Yes." I placed my hand in his and stood as he gently pulled me to my feet.

He sighed then, his lips forming a thin line I'd come to recognize as dread. "All right, Amanda. Seeing the battle was bad enough. Come with me, but don't say I didn't warn you." I walked beside him as he spoke to a large warrior across the room. "Trist, the command deck is yours."

"Yes, Sir. Lady Zakar, it's an honor."

"Thank you."

The giant warrior bowed to me as we walked past. Grigg led me out into the hallway, my hand safely in his warm touch. He made me feel safer just by the contact. I had to hope that he felt at least soothed by mine. "Where are we going?"

"To medical."

———

CONRAV, Medical Station One

I SHUDDERED as the two contaminated warriors that had survived their time on the Hive base arrived on field cots, rushed here from the shuttle.

We would try to save them. We *always* tried.

"Doctor Rhome?"

"I'm here." The cool-headed doctor had transferred here after his only son perished in battle in Sector 453. He was twenty years my senior, and he'd seen more Hive Integrations than I cared to think about. It was my goal, Grigg's goal, never to compare.

The two bodies twitched and fought the restraints that held them strapped to the exam tables. Two days ago, they'd been young Prillon warriors in their prime, lost on a scouting patrol. Now?

They were still warriors, but with no memory of their pasts, their identities wiped away by what had been described to me as a constant buzzing inside their minds. Like all warriors, they were large, and with their new Hive implants they would be stronger than any but our Atlan warriors in berserker mode, the microscopic bio-implants integrated into their muscular and nervous systems making them stronger, faster, and harder to kill than us inferior biologicals.

Fucking Hive.

"Which one do you want?"

Doctor Rhone shrugged. "I'll take the right."

I nodded and he stepped forward instructing the crew to wheel his patient toward the surgical station. I'd go left with my own crew and the warrior who still bore the dark orange collar of a Myntar mate around his neck.

Fuck. I knew him.

The door to the medical station slid open and I sensed who would be on the other side even before Grigg and Amanda stepped into the room. I motioned my surgical team to go ahead and prep the warrior at the station and glared at Grigg. "She has no business here. Are you fucking out of your mind?"

She wasn't a warrior, wasn't a doctor. She shouldn't see this pain, this disturbing reality of war.

Grigg's stare was cold, hard and completely unrelenting. "She needs to see what happens to us, what will happen to Earth."

"No." I turned to our mate, to the soft brown eyes, so innocent, so fucking stubborn. "No, Amanda. I won't allow it. You should not see this. I am speaking as your second, my only wish to protect you, to shield you from it all."

The contaminated warrior to my right bellowed and raged as the surgical team struggled to sedate him for extraction of the core processor the Hive had implanted. Amanda jumped at the sound and I shook my head at her. If the warrior survived, he'd be sent to The Colony to live out the rest of his life in peace.

Most did not survive.

I couldn't let her see this dark misery, didn't want her tainted by Hive filth. "No, Amanda."

"Please, Rav?" Her eyes were fervent. Eager, not to see the harshness of what the Hive did to us, but eager for the truth. "I need to see for myself."

"No," I repeated. My first instinct was to protect my mate, and there was no fucking way she was watching one of these motherfuckers die on the table.

Grigg growled and I knew I was going to hate the next words out of his mouth. I wasn't wrong. "Show her, Rav. That's an order."

"Fuck." I shook my head. "I fucking hate you right now."

"I know."

I couldn't look at him as I turned to my team. I ignored Amanda as well, she and Grigg following me like shadows.

The warrior had been strapped to the surgical table with special bonds we'd created just for this purpose. The Hive implants made them so fucking strong we'd had to develop special alloys to contain them.

The warrior Doctor Rhome had taken settled and I knew that his fate would be decided in the next few minutes. I dismissed him from my mind. He was in Doctor Rhome's hands now. I had my own patient to worry about.

The warrior on the table before me was covered with silver skin starting at his neck, up his face to his temples, but for some odd reason the Hive had left his forehead and hair alone. His left arm had been completely mechanized, the robotic compartments opening and closing as small gadgets and weapons searched for a target. His legs appeared to be normal, but there was no way to be sure until we'd stripped him naked and done a full inspection.

We wouldn't bother unless he survived the next five minutes.

"Sedate him, now."

"Yes, Doctor."

Amanda hovered near his feet and I couldn't look at her as my patient strained and cried out, the words an unintelligible jumble of sounds. The noise faded and the bio-monitors on the wall indicated his mind had settled into unconsciousness.

"Turn him." Four medical staff hurried to do as I bid, all of them faces I knew and trusted, faces who'd gone through this hell with me before. Again and again.

Looking over my shoulder, I signaled an unoccupied member of my staff to join us. The young woman, newly mated and still innocent of the horrors of this war, hurried to stand before me. "Yes, Doctor?"

"Please notify Captain Myntar, in person, that his second was recovered from the Hive Integration Unit and is being processed in med one." Captain Myntar would understand what wasn't said, and, if he was smart, would keep his mate, Mara, far, far from here for a while.

"He's on the command deck," Grigg added. "Damn it."

She hurried to do as I bid, to deliver the news to our third in command as Amanda raised her hand to cover her mouth. "Myntar?"

"Yes."

Amanda gasped and I turned to her.

"Are you all right?"

"Yes, it's just—Mara. I know her. She's the one... He's Mara's mate?"

I lifted my gaze to Grigg's and he nodded. The time for secrets or half-truths was over. I softened my tone when I answered her. "Yes, mate. This is Mara's second."

"Oh, God."

Grigg led her to the edge of the small surgical area, his arm supporting her waist as I returned my full attention to the warrior whose life hung in the balance. Now lying on his side, my team had cut away the armor covering his spine. The new scar was easily visible, the mark nearly five inches long running the left edge of his spine, not far from his heart.

"Bio-integrity field?" I asked as I took my place at his back.

"Activated and fully operational, Doctor."

The energy field surrounding his body would prevent infection or cross contamination when we opened him up. I rolled my shoulders slightly, trying to ease the tension pinching me like microscopic vices. Some days I fucking hated my job. This wasn't being a doctor, healing the sick, this was being a butcher, and oftentimes, a killer.

I didn't shoot Hive scouts of the air or tear them apart with my bare hands on the battlefield, but I caused the death of more than my share, right here in a room designed to heal. And the real mind-fuck was every single one of them would probably thank me if they could.

Someone handed me a pair of surgical gloves and I slipped my hands into them as another placed the ion-blade on a waist-high tray to my left. Cutting was barbaric, beyond cruel, and the only way to remove the foreign objects the Hive implanted in our warriors, our women, our fucking children.

"All right, let's get the damn thing out of him."

"He's stable."

I nodded and reached for the ion-blade. Lifting the device to Myntar's back, I cut him open slowly, layer by layer until the bones that lined his spinal column came into view. But I knew that wouldn't be enough. I kept cutting away the bone until I saw what I hunted, the silver orb attached to his spinal cord, countless microscopic tendrils working their way through his nerves, working their way up and down his spinal cord, weaving themselves into his system. Taking him over.

We called the strange device their core processor, for any Hive, from the lowest scout to their fiercest soldier classes, ceased to function without it. Once removed, the minds of the individuals became their own, the constant buzzing chatter they suffered as part of the collective, silenced.

There was no easy way to remove it. Over the centuries we'd tried everything. Cutting. Tearing, Ripping it free. Melting the metal. It didn't matter how gentle or unforgiving our method, the result was the same.

The man either lived or he died in a matter of minutes, a self-destruct sequence activated by the remaining implants that had been spread throughout the rest of the victim's body. It wasn't pretty, nor free of pain for the victim.

"I see it, Doctor."

"Yes." I set the blade down and dug my fingers deep into the warrior's exposed flesh, wrapped my fingers around the metal orb that was a quarter the size of my fist. "Everyone ready?"

A chorus of yeses sounded around me as I gritted my teeth and pulled. Hard.

manda

GRIGG'S ARM was the only thing keeping me on my feet. Mara's *mate*. Little Lan's second father. Her family was about to shatter right before my eyes and I couldn't help but imagine the wrenching pain of losing one of my mates, of seeing Grigg or Rav so helpless and broken on that table.

I didn't know exactly what they were doing to the Prillon warrior, but by the tension in the air and grim faces around the room, I knew it wasn't anything good. I ignored the sounds of the second medical team working across the room on another warrior who probably had a family. Loved ones. I didn't want to know. I had all I could deal with right here.

That the man was a Prillon warrior was obvious by his golden hair, sharp features and dark gold forehead. But below that his skin had been altered to a strange, shimmering silver. Before they'd knocked him out his entire left arm had looked like something out of a robot horror movie, strange little devices emerging from his flesh to click, or grasp, or buzz into empty space like a lost fly repeatedly bashing its body against a clear window trying to get back outdoors.

The whole thing was so strange and sad. "What did they do to him?" I whispered my question to Grigg as Rav was completely focused on his patient and I did not want to distract him.

"They consume other races, implant us with technology that regulates our bodies. The core processor Rav is removing from his back integrates with the spinal cord. It's a biosynthetic that continues to grow and expand with time until it infiltrates the brain. After that, there's no hope at all."

"I don't understand." I refused to look away as Rav cut open the warrior's back. I even leaned closer as the light silver shimmer of a foreign object became visible where it had somehow attached itself to the man's spine. *The core processor.* It looked wholly alien, so much more sinister than anything I'd ever seen.

Grigg's hand came to rest on the back of my neck and I crossed my arms over my chest, bracing for the revulsion I knew was coming.

"Rav is going to remove it. Once he does that, we'll know in the next few minutes."

"Know what?"

"He'll either wake up from his stupor and remember who he is, in which case he'll be rushed to a ReGen pod to repair the damage to his spine."

"Or?" I nudged Grigg with my shoulder, even as I leaned into the strong fingers massaging the base of my neck.

"Or he'll self-destruct."

I gasped. "What?"

What the hell did that mean? I opened my mouth to ask another question but all thought fled as I watched Rav's muscles bulge and flex as he braced himself against the edge of the table and yanked the silver orb from the warrior's back with one violent twist of his forearm.

"Containment!" Rav barked the order and one of his helpers in gray rushed forward with a small black box. Rav dropped the silver orb inside, the hairlike tendrils waving in the air as if searching for another host, another body to invade.

That thing was creepier than the worst of the monster-sized cockroaches I'd found under the sink of my crap apartment in college.

The officer closed the lid and rushed to an S-Gen station in the center of the medical station. He hurriedly placed his hand on the scanner and I sighed with relief when the bright green light flared and the box, and the creepy silver orb, disappeared, I had to hope, forever.

I turned back to find Rav finishing up, running a small ReGen wand over the cut he'd made in the warrior's back. "Time?"

"Two minutes."

Rav looked so sad, so resigned, and I knew from the anger and helplessness I felt flowing through my collar that Rav didn't think the warrior was going to survive. "Roll him onto his back. Let's see if he wakes up."

They scrambled to do as Rav bid and I bit my lip, waiting to see what would happen next. The gadgets on the warrior's arm remained dormant and I wondered what would happen to them if he survived.

Rav looked at me then, his gaze, unlike Grigg's, hid nothing from me. He let me see everything, the pain, the helpless rage, the regret that he couldn't do more. I could *feel* it.

"If he survives, I'll remove as much as I can. But most of the damage is microscopic, biological implants too small to track or remove will have been embedded in his muscles, his bones, his eyes and skin, all designed to make him stronger, faster, his sight keener, his flesh resistant to extremes of temperature."

"Is he—may I—" Hell, I wasn't sure exactly what I wanted to say, but I wanted to get a closer look.

Grigg deferred to Rav, who nodded. He sighed, probably realizing he could no longer protect me from the worst. "Go ahead, Amanda. Get a good look at what the Hive can do."

I stepped forward, my legs stiff and unsteady at first, but I waved away Grigg's offer to assist. I wanted to see this for myself. I needed to see this.

Four steps, five, and I was beside the hulking mass of the unconscious warrior. He looked almost peaceful, his strange silver face in repose. I wandered the edges of the exam table, taking it all in, the strange metallic pieces attached to his arm, the silver hue of his skin, the complete lack of recognition or control he'd possessed before they'd put him under. He'd been insane, incoherent. Unrecognizable as—as what? I'd been thinking as a human being, but he wasn't human, was he?

He was alien. A Prillon warrior who just a few days ago I would have called enemy. Invader. Shake-down artist.

But he was a mate to Mara. A father. A family man. A warrior who wanted peace just as much as any soldier on Earth.

Shame swirled in my heart as I realized just how fucking small Earth truly was, and how much smaller still our superstitious, frightened intellects.

I lifted my gaze to each of my mates and let my regret, my understanding flow to each of them through our shared bond. "I'm so sorry. I had no idea."

They both shifted, as if trying to decide exactly what to say to me now that I was no longer fighting them, no longer resisting the truth of my new life. Seeing Mara's mate solidified this. Whatever Earth's doubts were, they were no longer mine. I knew the truth. I saw it firsthand. I believed the Coalition. I believed my mates.

I would need to contact the agency as soon as possible, let them know what was going on out here. The truth.

The comm unit in medical beeped, followed by a voice I recognized as that of Captain Trist. "Commander, we need you on deck. We've got Hive scout ships coming at us from three systems."

Grigg looked at me and I nodded, waving him away. I was fine. They needed him to keep us all safe. While Rav saved lives in the medical unit, Grigg saved lives by commanding, leading. Running the ship, the squadron. All of us.

"Go. They need you."

He nodded once, then turned on his heel and left me with Rav.

The saved warrior moved, a soft groan leaving his throat as I leaned over him. His eyes flickered open and I felt my own gaze widen at the bright glimmer of silver that ringed his irises, the effect similar to photos I'd seen of a solar eclipse.

"Mara." The warrior called for his mate, but his gaze was squarely on me, and I looked nothing like the tall, orange-and-golden female who belonged to him.

"She's coming."

"Mara!" His back arched and instinctively I reached for his hand to offer comfort. His grip nearly crushed my fingers, but I held firm and placed my free hand on his forehead.

"Shhh. You're okay. Mara is coming."

"Mara." He went limp as I held him, his gaze locked on my face but seeing another's as I stroked the hair from his forehead in what I hoped was a soothing caress.

A shudder raced from his spine, extending to his limbs and suddenly Rav was there, pulling me backward, away from the warrior who twisted and contorted with pain on the table.

"What's happening to him?"

"He's dying." Rav settled me against his chest but didn't force me to turn away. I *couldn't* look away as the gadgets lining his arm oozed like someone had pumped acid into the metal, cooking it off his body from the inside out. His flesh bubbled and churned as well, as if he were boiling on the inside.

Nausea rose and I choked back bile as his rib cage collapsed, his chest imploded in some horrific scene I'd never imagined existed outside a horror movie. Tears streaked down my face and Rav lifted me off my feet, finally turning me away, placing his big, warm, safe body between me and the dreadful story playing out on the table behind him. "All right, Amanda, that's enough."

I breathed him in, shaking like a leaf. I'd wanted to know, and now I did. God help me.

The smell of the warrior's churning flesh clogged my head and I gagged, grasping desperately at Rav's uniform. "I can't breathe."

"Get him out of here before his mates arrive." Rav gave the order over his shoulder as he shuffled me out of the room. Before we reached the door I stumbled and he swooped me up, cradling me in his arms as he carried me back toward the small exam room where I'd first met him and Grigg.

By the time the door closed behind us, I was shaking.

"Hush, mate. It's all right."

"He...he bubbled."

Rav cursed. "I'm sorry, Amanda. I tried to warn you."

And he had, my compassionate Rav. He had argued with Grigg, tried to keep the sight from me. He'd known how bad it would be, they both had.

Rav sat in a chair, settling me across his lap as I tried to focus on his scent, his heat, the strength of the arms that held me tightly to him. I gripped his shirt, held on, as if he would anchor me. I breathed him in until my stomach settled and I could think again.

"No. I needed to know. I had to see for myself." I reached up and placed a tender kiss on his neck, wrapping my arms around his waist, pressing my cheek to his chest as I held him close. Squeezed him, afraid he would set me aside and return to his duty, as Grigg had been forced to do. So many people depended on my mates. And what was I? Nothing. A distraction. A weak female who, right now, would sell her soul if that's what it took to be held by one of her mates, just like this.

Perhaps I had, sold my soul, that is. I hadn't been matched because I'd wanted mates. I'd been matched because I was a spy. I'd been one for years. But as I held Rav, I realized I truly had lost my soul somewhere along the way. I had nothing and no one in my life. I'd been married to my job, unable to trust, unwilling to risk being hurt. But now, now I had Grigg and Rav, and Rav felt *so* very good and solid and real. So much better than the cold comfort of the United States government.

"How many times have you had to go through that? Does it happen a lot?"

"Watching a good man die?"

"Yes."

"Myntar was number two-hundred and seventy-three. But most who are taken by the Hive are never recovered. We end up fighting them on the field of battle, not here, in a medical station," Rav grumbled, as my mind reeled—he kept track? Each life so precious that he never wanted to forget? "And I'm not happy you had to see it even once."

I sighed, then breathed him in. "I know. I'm sorry I'm so stubborn. I'm sorry. I'm nobody, Rav. So many people need you, you and Grigg. I shouldn't even be here. I'm just a distraction for you. A pain in the ass you don't need. God, I'm sorry. For everything."

Rav lifted his hand to my neck, his giant palm sliding under my jaw and gently raising my face to his. "Never apologize again. You are perfect. I love your fire, your strong mind. I need you, mate. Grigg needs you. Before you, we were both lost."

They were lost? That was almost laughable. They had purpose.

"No, Rav. You're both so strong, so much responsibility on your shoulders. You don't need me here, distracting you. I've been such an idiot. All I've done is make things worse, more complicated, for both of you."

His lips lowered to mine, lingered in a soft caress more reverent than sexual. His mouth was soft and warm, gentle. Tears filled my eyes as his complete devotion, adoration and a desperate longing to be loved filled me through our connection. He was hurting from Myntar's death, too, but didn't show it. I had the luxury of the collar to make me aware of his pain, of his need for me, I was the one to ease him, to love him.

"Conrav." I whispered his name, lifting my arms to bury my fingers in his hair as I pulled him to me, pulled his face to my neck, cuddling him as I sensed he needed, my huge warrior mate. He did need me, he'd not simply said the words to soothe me or convince me to stay.

I held him close, running my fingers through his hair over and over in a soothing gesture, loving him the best I could. His pale gold hair was like tiny strands of silk between my fingers. "Your hair is so soft."

That earned me a chuckle as his gentle hands slid up and down my spine in a comforting glide. "I need you, Amanda. We both need you. Neither of us are good at expressing our feelings with words. So thank the gods for the collars." He kissed me. "Yes, I love fucking you, I love your body, your wet pussy, the sounds you make when we're loving you, but it's so much more than that. I need you like this, soft and gentle. I need to feel your love around me soothing the fires that rage in my soul. To heal me, even when I'm not truly hurt. I need to hold you and be still, just like this. Grigg needs it too, even more than I do. His rage is like a volcano inside him. We need you. Gods, please, Amanda. You can't leave us."

I'd never considered staying forever, even when I knew I couldn't go home, my mind hadn't wrapped around the idea of committing to my mates, of choosing them. But they'd just given me everything I'd asked for, everything I needed to be free, to make my own choice. For years now my life had been my job and nothing but the job. I'd had no options. But now, the choice was clear. And in that moment I knew, beyond a shadow of a doubt, exactly what that choice was going to be.

"I'm not going anywhere. You're mine, Rav. You and Grigg are mine." My voice was stronger now that I was resolved. Sure. "I need to contact Earth, tell them what I've seen here. They need to know the truth."

"They won't listen." Rav lifted his head from my shoulder and met my gaze. "We tried to tell them. We showed them cadavers of warriors like Myntar, showed them images of battles, of Hive scouts, their Integration Units. All of it."

I stiffened, rage rising to choke me. "You what?" They'd told me none of this. Cadavers? Video of Hive installations and ships, of Hive soldiers in active combat.

"We gave them all the proof they could need. They aren't interested in listening."

While I didn't want to believe it, I knew Rav spoke the truth. I didn't need the surety of his words coming through the collar to make me believe. "If they had the proof, then why did they send me out here? What do they want?"

Rav placed a gentle kiss on my lips, his gaze cloudy. "I don't know, mate. You tell me."

Oh, I knew all right. Weapons. They wanted weapons. Technology. Anything that would get them ahead in their battle for domination of our little blue planet. My presence here wasn't about the Coalition at all, or the arrival of the spacemen. It was all about Earth's petty wars, the never-ceasing struggle for power.

After what I'd just witnessed, their obsessive struggle for

supremacy was laughable. There was so much more out here, so much more that humans, with their petty fighting, had yet to comprehend. "When do Earth's first soldiers arrive?"

"Soon. Tomorrow."

Holy shit. I didn't have much time. "I want to meet them first, talk to them. And..." My voice faded as I considered what I could do to convince the soldiers arriving from Earth that the threat was real.

"And?"

"I want them to see Myntar's body. I want them to watch what happened. Do you have the video on file? Are there cameras in the medical station?"

Rav groaned and I felt his utter and complete disgust at the idea. "Everything that happens on this ship is recorded."

Everything? Shit. They hadn't exactly told me that either. But that was a concern for another day. "Let me show them, Rav. I know these guys, their type. They live by a code of honor that's solid. Their loyalty is absolute. They'll listen to me."

"I hope so. I truly hope so. Because if they so much as glare at you, if Grigg believes they are a threat, he will kill them."

I shuddered, knowing Rav spoke true. Grigg's patience had been pushed to the breaking point by me, by Earth's bullshit attitude and the day's losses to the Hive. "They won't."

"Good. But you should know, love, if Earth tries to fuck with the Coalition's fleet, they'll lose."

"Would the Interstellar Coalition let the Hive take us out? Destroy Earth?" The idea was terrifying, but I had no idea what the Prime of Rav's home world, or the leaders of the other planets, might decide if Earth's leaders didn't get their heads out of their asses. Earth was so small, and so very, very far away.

"No. We'll protect them, even if they don't deserve it. There are billions of innocents on your world who need to be sheltered."

"But what about our soldiers? You know Earth's leaders

won't stop trying to get their hands on a weapon. A human pilot could easily steal a ship. Why let them come here at all? I don't understand."

Rav stroked my cheek as he explained. "You must understand, we are very, very far away from your home. Should a human pilot steal a ship, he would never make it out of this system alive. The light of your star takes thousands of years to reach us. There are over two hundred and sixty member planets in the coalition, most in different solar systems. The Fleet protects trillions of beings, hundreds of worlds separated by vast expanses of space. We live and fight and die and most never leave their sector of space. We are a vast network spread out over unimaginable distances connected only by our transport technology."

"Then, how did I get here?"

"Our transport system uses the gravity wells around stars and black holes to accelerate travel and communications. You journeyed here as a beam of pure energy accelerated to speeds you can not comprehend. Our transport and communications stations are very secure and guarded by entire battle groups of warriors. Your naïve human spies could not break into our system even if we walked them through the door and chained them to the controls. The transport pads are controlled by bioscanners and neurostim units implanted directly in the brain of our technicians. There is no way for your people to overcome our security. Even the Hive has been unable to do so, and their race is much more advanced than the humans of Earth."

"So, there's truly nothing Earth can do and no way to send anything back without permission, not even a simple message?"

"No. There is not. But your Earth is not the first world to doubt our intentions. Your leaders will come around eventually. They always do." Rav kissed me again and I melted in his arms, our embrace one of comfort and care, not hot monkey sex, although Rav was pretty damn good at that, too.

"I love you, Amanda. Whatever happens, I want you to know that."

I didn't have the words, not yet, but I held him close for a long time, both of us lost in our own thoughts, the connection between us wide open and flooded with tenderness, with love, as I allowed myself to believe he was mine to keep, allowed myself to fall absolutely, no-holds-barred, head-over-heels in love with him.

14

G *rigg*

THE DINING HALL was full and the crowd of people who stopped to greet Amanda had begun to grate on my nerves. In less than an hour, the first soldiers from Earth would arrive via transport, and my beautiful, soft-hearted little mate had somehow convinced me not to kill them.

"Lady Zakar, Commander, Doctor." Captain Trist bowed low as he rose from the opposite side of the round table, his tray now empty. "I must report to the command deck."

"Captain." I inclined my head as he left us. I often took my meals here, but before Amanda's arrival, most had simply nodded silently and passed me by. Today I felt like the center of a one-woman event.

Everyone wanted to meet our mate, greet her, offer their congratulations. Amanda took it all in stride, seated as she was between myself on her right and Rav on her left. No one got close enough to touch. I was still too raw from the events of yesterday to let her out of my sight, mine or Rav's.

I'd felt them bonding, soothing each other, the peaceful flood of emotion soothing me as far away as the command deck where I'd sent more than a hundred pilots into battle. We'd lost a dozen, but the Hive incursion had been pushed back.

The war went on. And on. And fucking on. I'd been fighting since I was a boy, my father dragging me with him to the command deck when I was a mere child, teaching me strategy. Teaching me how to deliver the killing blow, how to kill without mercy. Twenty years I'd been fighting, and each death took a toll on my soul. I was battered, worn down.

Before Amanda, I had forced myself to fight for duty, for honor. Now? Now I fought for her, and my determination to drive back the Hive forces, to protect her and all of my people, settled like a mountain in my chest, unmoving and without mercy. For her, I could fight forever.

She pushed the food around on her plate, an expression of distaste on her beautiful face, and I realized that I had not thought to find out what the people of Earth liked to eat.

"I'm sorry, Amanda. I should have thought to order dishes from Earth for the S-Gen programmers. I will remedy that immediately."

She leaned her head against my shoulder, touching me with a comfort and familiarity I was quickly coming to crave. "It's all right, Grigg. You've got much more important things to deal with than my taste buds."

"No, love. I don't. You are the only thing that matters to me." I meant it. If I lost her, I'd have no reason to keep fighting. I'd be finished.

Her eyes widened when I failed to hold back my emotion, but I was done hiding the ferocity of my devotion, my need, from her. Rav shifted in his seat as I was sure he felt it, too, the link forged by our collars both a blessing and a curse. I simply glowered at him, daring him to say a word.

Which, of course, he did.

"Told you, love."

She smiled and her smile morphed to a small laugh. "Yes, you did."

I held her face still between my palms and kissed her once. Twice. Right there in front of everyone as an unnatural hush fell over the room. "What did he tell you?" I whispered.

Amanda's secretive smile was all feminine mystery and I longed to throw her down on the table and fuck the truth out of her.

Gods, I needed to get control of myself, but knew I wouldn't be able to rein in my dominant nature, not until she was safely ours forever, the claiming ceremony complete, her collar a dark midnight blue.

Rav saved me from making a fool of myself in the middle of the fucking dining room. "I told her you were a pathetic, needy mess."

I considered denying his words, but the soft glow in Amanda's eyes, the total acceptance I saw in her gaze, stopped me cold. She knew. She already fucking knew the truth. "Yes, I am."

Admitting it didn't make me weaker. It didn't make me anything my father said I would become. Instead, it made me stronger, for I knew Amanda and Rav would be there for me, supporting me, encouraging me. Loving me, no matter what hardship we faced.

The confession earned me another smile and a sigh that made me feel like I'd just conquered the entire Hive collective. I kissed her again, pulling her as close as I dared in such a public place. When I let her go, she smiled and turned to Rav, kissing him, too, making sure he knew what he meant to her.

Glowing with happiness, she forced another bite of the

nutrient-rich protein cubes down, her eyes scanning the crowd that had suddenly found something else to do, and somewhere else to look. But the room *felt* lighter, calmer, happier.

Maybe that was just me.

Amanda gasped and jumped to her feet. I rose instantly, Rav a split second slower, both of us ready to tear the head off whatever had scared her, but it wasn't panic flooding my collar, it was sorrow.

Confused, I looked down at my mate as she placed a hand on my arm to stay me before walking away, toward a couple and small boy that had just entered the dining room.

Silence descended as my mate approached Captain Myntar and his mate, everyone watching, waiting to see what Amanda was going to do.

She didn't say a word, but her gaze locked with the much larger Prillon female's for scant seconds before Mara leaned forward, collapsing with heaving sobs in Amanda's outstretched arms.

As if a dam had broken, everyone in the dining hall rose and surrounded Myntar and his mate and child, offering support and sharing in their sorrow. My little human mate was in the center of the small crowd, cementing my people into a family unit stronger than it had ever been.

"Gods, she's going to fucking kill me with that soft heart of hers." Rav was rubbing his chest, trying to alleviate the sharp, stabbing ache I knew he must be feeling, because Amanda's pain was our pain, and she was truly broken-hearted for Mara and Myntar and little Lan.

"We didn't have a heart before her," I said.

"Agreed." Rav twisted and turned his head on his shoulders, cracking his spine to relieve some tension. "I've got to get to medical and prepare the body." He turned to me. "You sure about this?"

"Yes. And so is she."

Rav nodded, patting me on the shoulder as he walked past. "I'll see you down there."

I followed behind and waited patiently beside him for the crowd to clear so we could reach the small family at its center.

"I'm sorry, my friends." I patted the captain on the shoulder and bowed to Lady Myntar as Rav came up next to me, his sorrow clearly etched on his face. He'd spoken to the couple the night before, when he'd had to explain to them exactly what had happened. Rav had come back to our room looking ragged and raw and crawled into Amanda's arms.

Mara released my mate and wiped the tears from her eyes to look at us. "We know there was nothing to be done, but thank you all." She looked at the faces surrounding her, offering support, led by their new Lady, the new heart of the battle group. "Thank you. I'm proud to be a Prillon bride." Her gaze drifted to Amanda as she continued, "And happy to call you friend."

Amanda squeezed her hand one last time and walked to us, her mates, where we waited for her and I realized I would always wait for her, always protect her, always love her. I took her hand as we followed Rav from the room and thanked the gods for the matching protocols that had brought her to me, my perfect match, my mate.

———

Amanda

I waited silently at the front of the meeting room Grigg told me was normally used for meetings of the battle wings before a mission. Twelve long tables with three chairs behind them in classroom style faced the front of the room where a giant communications monitor was imbedded in the wall.

When I was ready, all I had to do was ask to be patched through to Robert and Allen back on Earth. I had no idea how their communications worked across such vast expanses of space, and I didn't care. All I knew was I could talk to them in real time and try to make them see reason.

I'd warned Grigg that they wouldn't listen, that their focus was solely on Earth and the bickering there, so he'd suggested I make contact with the Coalition's Planetary Induction teams and explain to them Earth's subterfuge. I'd sat beside him this morning on my first deep-space version of a teleconference and explained the fears and doubts of the people I worked for to a council of mixed races and strange beings I could barely comprehend. They'd listened attentively, from light years away, and were on standby to relieve the much more diplomatic representatives of the Coalition that were now trying, in vain, to deal with Earth's hard-headed leaders.

I told them everything I knew, trusting Grigg and these strangers who held the fate of all humanity in the palms of their hands. If I doubted, all I need do was recall the memory of Myntar's bubbling flesh, his cries of pain as the Hive implants in his body killed him. When I thought of that happening to all the innocent citizens of Earth, I straightened my spine and squared my shoulders. I had to protect my people, even if they didn't understand what I was doing.

The door slid open and Grigg walked in, Rav directly behind him and immediately I went to my mates, grateful as their arms wrapped around me, enclosing me so that I felt safe and loved, stronger with them beside me.

"Are they here?" I asked.

Grigg sighed. "Yes. They are going through processing now. Then we'll take them to medical, and they'll be all yours."

"How long will that take?"

"About twenty minutes. We aren't giving them the full

exam, just making sure they're healthy enough to survive their return trip."

Grigg had ensured the transporter was ready to send them back. He was willing for me to meet with the Earth soldiers, but refused to allow them to remain. They would learn the truth, see Myntar's body, the recording of his death, then go back and report what they'd seen. They would serve the Coalition better in this task alone than fighting the Hive for their two-year service time.

I nodded, pulling from their arms. I wiped my clammy palms on the thighs of my dark blue uniform, proud to be wearing the color of my family, and prouder still of the new insignia on my left shoulder. Grigg had officially named me Lady Zakar and updated the ship's systems to allow me access to everything, including ship's systems, weapons, histories, medical information. Everything I could possibly need to betray him. His trust in me, in *us*, was substantial. He'd done it, then kissed me senseless. I could now issue orders to everyone in the battle group, everyone but him.

Which was just fine with me. His dominant, bossy ways made me shiver with anticipation, for as soon as this was done, as soon as the Earthmen learned the truth and were sent back, we would complete the mating ceremony. I'd told them I was ready, that while we'd told each other of our love, felt it through the collar, the bonding ceremony would make it official. I wanted my collar the color of theirs. I wanted to belong to them forever, just as my mates would belong to me.

"Let's get this over with so I can claim you." I purposely reminded them of what was to come and was rewarded with a flood of heat through my collar. Both men glanced at me with heated stares, stares that were promises of their own need to finalize their claim.

"Commander Zakar?" The communications officer's voice filled the room.

"Yes?"

"General Zakar is requesting to speak to you, Sir."

Grigg sighed, his hand coming up to rub the back of his neck and Rav's eyes narrowed in irritation. Curious now, I was glad when Grigg gave the order to patch his father through to the monitor at the front of the room.

"Commander?"

"Yes, General?" Grigg stepped forward, to the center of the room so his father could easily see him as I studied the much older Prillon warrior on the screen. His features were similar to Grigg's, but the general's coloring was much darker, his skin a burnished gold that was almost copper in color, his hair a dark shade of burnt orange. The uniform he wore was one I recognized, the armor of a warrior, but no longer black, but the same blue hue of mine, Zakar blue.

"How dare you keep your mate a secret from me. I had to hear about her from the medical staff."

Grigg's jaw tightened and I felt the tension pouring from him in waves, the anger. "My mate was never a secret, Father, I simply didn't realize you'd care."

The general leaned forward, squinting to get a good look at me where I stood near the back of the room. I looked at Rav, who shrugged and spoke to me low enough so that the monitors wouldn't pick up his voice. "Go ahead if you want, but he's an asshole."

That sealed it for me. I wasn't going to allow my Grigg to stand alone. Not anymore. I walked forward, head held high and slipped my hand into Grigg's much larger one. The general inspected me and I looked back. He was nothing to me, and if he hurt my mate, he was my enemy. Still, this was my father-in-law. Manners required I attempt to be polite. "General. It's a pleasure to meet you."

He took his time looking me over, as if he were inspecting a breeding mare for his prize stallion. "She'll do, although I wish you had chosen a Prillon mate."

"She was matched to me through the Bride Program. I assume you acknowledge their success rate. That should be enough to satisfy you. To me, she's my matched mate. I would have no other."

His father crossed his arms with a harrumph and scowled. "Fine, Commander. Fuck whomever you want. I don't care as long as she breeds. I will transport immediately for the claiming ceremony."

Behind me, Rav growled.

Um, yeah. No. There was no way my father-in-law was going to watch the claiming ceremony. Gross and altogether creepy.

His protest fell on deaf ears as Grigg's rage boiled over. Gently, too gently, he stepped forward and used his arm to move me behind his back, out of his father's sight. "No."

"What did you say to me?"

Grigg's entire body tensed with rage and I stayed where he wanted me, content to lean against him, to press my forehead to the center of his back so he'd know I was there, that I was with him. "I said no, Father. No more."

I heard a rustling and felt Rav's approach as he walked to Grigg's side, standing with Grigg as he refused his father.

"What are you talking about? No more? What the fuck kind of game are you playing with me, boy?"

I expected Grigg to explode in wild rage, was shocked when the opposite occurred. It was like all the anger drained out of him, leaving him calm and relaxed. "Amanda is my mate and I will not subject her to your presence. I am done with you. I'm your blood, and I will always honor our family. But I am not your son, and you are not welcome on my ship. If you have need to communicate with me again, you may send a message via my communications officer. I have no desire to speak with you ever again."

The general raged, but Grigg simply lifted walked forward and placed his palm on a small command pad. The room went blessedly silent.

I followed him, wrapping my arms around Grigg from behind as Rav's sense of satisfaction mingled with Grigg's resignation. "About fucking time."

"Yes, it was." Grigg's hands settled over mine atop his abdomen and I squeezed. I didn't completely understand what had just happened, but based on my mates' reactions, it was a good thing, and had been a long time coming.

I wanted to ask but the sound of men speaking—in English!—reached my ears and I released my hold on my mates to battle my own demons.

As we'd planned, I walked to the front of the room where I could be seen by all of the spec-ops soldiers who'd just arrived from Earth. They entered and seated themselves at the tables, their eyes dark, their expressions grim. About what I'd expected. They were SEALS and Rangers, spooks and assassins. But I knew by the cautious look on more than one face that Myntar's mangled body had not been what they'd expected to see in their first hour in deep space.

Welcome to the front lines, boys.

Grigg and Rav moved to the front wall, one on each side of the giant monitor where they offered me their silent support. They were leaving this to me, thank God, because Grigg's idea of diplomacy was torturing each and every man for information before sending them all back to Earth in body bags.

It had taken me nearly half an hour to talk him out of it, but he had a point. Earth was part of the Interstellar Coalition now, and we were either "in" or we were "out". There was no middle ground, not when the Hive threat loomed to destroy us all.

When they were seated and the door closed, I turned to

face them and seeing so many human faces again felt strange. They looked...alien.

"Gentlemen, I assume you have questions?"

I spent the next hour telling them exactly who I was, who I worked for, the mission I'd been assigned and everything I'd learned since. They'd watched the recording of Myntar's death, seen his body, watched replays of several battles and been shown video and statistics on Hive movements, numbers, and just how long this war had been going on...over a thousand years.

When I was done, I looked each man in the eye and held his gaze. "I know for a fact that at least two of you were sent here for the same reason I was, under direct orders from the Director to gather intel and get your hands on any weaponry, technology or information the agency might find useful." I tapped my foot as I leaned forward, my palms flat on the table directly in front of me. "But now, like me, you know the truth. You've seen the threat with your own eyes. Care to come forward?"

When the room remained silent, as I'd expected, I nodded at Grigg to let him know I was ready. He ordered comms to patch through my call. Behind me the screen lit up with a scene from home, Robert and Allen seated around a small table with a man I recognized as the Secretary of Defense.

15

I TURNED TO FACE THEM. "GENTLEMEN."

"Miss Bryant, what's the meaning of this? We've been waiting here for over an hour. Why are you contacting us? We were expecting to speak to an officer of the Zakar battle group."

I resisted the urge to roll my eyes, barely. So unladylike, but Robert's false concern, his attempt to play the confused and befuddled official, rubbed me raw. For years I'd believed his every word, now I could see him for what he was. A self-serving bureaucrat that would do anything for personal or professional gain.

"I am Lady Zakar, of the Battle Group Zakar, a proud warrior bride of Prillon Prime. And Robert? I no longer work for you." I spread my hand out behind me in an arc, as if showing off the men seated behind me. "These men know the truth, gentlemen, and they'll be coming home on the next transport. They've seen the bodies, seen what the Hive can do, as have I."

Robert was sputtering, but it was the SecDef who silenced him, his gaze level and all business. "What is the purpose of this call?"

I wanted to punch him in the face for being so damn stubborn, so fucking stupid, but I understood. He was a man trying to do his job, a man who'd spent decades defending his country, and that was a deep, deep well, an engrained way of thinking very difficult to escape. Earth was his problem. Not space. At least not until now.

"Mr. Secretary, I was sent as the first bride to ascertain the extent of the Hive threat to Earth and to discover both the strength and intention of the Interstellar Coalition's Fleet to either protect or conquer our planet."

"And what have you discovered?"

"The Hive threat is very real, and would be impossible for us to survive. Without Coalition protection, we would be looking at complete annihilation of the entire human race in a matter of months."

"And you know this for a fact."

I nodded once. "Yes, Sir. I do."

My conviction startled him, and I watched the wheels in his head spin behind the reflective surface of his glasses as he considered the truth of my words, the implications. But I wasn't finished with him yet.

"What I would like to know, Sir, is how you all could be so damn stubborn as to send me on this mission when what you should be doing is recruiting and training soldiers to help save our planet."

"We have the strongest military in the world—"

I cut him off before he could spew the usual propaganda. "Yes, in the world, on Earth. You aren't in Kansas anymore. I know the Coalition presented you with contaminated cadavers,

battle recordings, information on the Hive systems and territory. But since you have not responded appropriately to the
Coalition's requests for honesty and cooperation, I have
contacted the Planetary Induction team. They will be arriving
on Earth in three days' time to straighten you out."

The SecDef's cheeks turned red and I realized he truly
didn't know what I was talking about. His next words
confirmed my suspicions. "What cadavers?"

I raised a brow. "Ask Allen."

Allen, the weasel, slammed his palm down on the table
before him. "Damn it. What the fuck are you doing?"

I smiled then, and I hoped it showed my disgust with his
petty, small-minded ways. "Saving you from yourself. Your
combat team will be transport ready in three hours. And the
next batch of soldiers you send us better be honorable
warriors, not spies."

With a wave of my hand I signaled the communications
officer to end the transmission.

The screen went blank and I took a deep breath, relief and
satisfaction stealing the tension from my limbs. On either side
of the screen my mates stood like guardian angels, there to
support me, love me, trust me to do what needed to be done, to
say what needed to be said to convince Earth's peoples to join
the fight in earnest.

My mates. I'd made my decision, and I'd chosen my men,
my future was here. I was a citizen of Prillon Prime, a member
of the clan Zakar. Grigg and Rav? Mine. And I wasn't giving
them up.

I spun to face the human soldiers still seated in the room,
on their faces a mixture of anger, resignation, confusion. I
knew exactly what they were going through. They were trying
to come to terms with the fact that they'd been lied to, used.
And, like me, they were loyal, honorable servants who'd
believed they were truly doing the right thing. The truth we'd

shown them in the last few hours was going to take time to digest.

"Gentlemen, when you see Allen, will one of you please punch him in the face and tell him it's from me?"

A large man near the door grinned at my request. "Consider it done."

"Thank you. Now, all of you, get out. Go home, and tell everyone the truth."

―――――

FIVE HOURS LATER...

CONRAV

MY COCK HAD BEEN hard for so long it hurt, and still Grigg had delayed our claiming ceremony, refusing to perform such a sacred right with traitors and spies among us.

I understood the emotion behind that decision, for standing there listening to the human men from Earth argue with our Amanda had made me eager to transport to Earth and beat some sense, and a healthy dose of respect for my mate, into their thick skulls. But Amanda had handled them with ease, and the pride I'd felt had been mirrored in Grigg.

She was truly the Lady Zakar now, tales of her compassion for Mara and her defiance of the human leaders making her legend already. Those who had yet to meet her were making up excuses to transport to the battleship, hoping to see her, or speak to her. The increase in transport requests had made Grigg laugh, but as always, Grigg had an answer for everything.

"*We'll announce formal welcoming celebrations aboard each*

ship. *If the crew wants to meet her, we'll have to take her to them. My battleship won't hold five thousand curious males."*

Worse, the number of males who had indicated an interest in bearing witness to our claiming had tripled in the last half hour. Their numbers were a sign of respect for our mating, for the rightness of our union, but I'd shared Amanda with the world enough for one day. Right now, I wanted her naked and eager for my cock. I wanted to watch her eyes glaze as Grigg guided our loving with a heavy hand.

Grigg and I escorted her to the center of the round room, all three of us naked and ready, Grigg on her right as I gently held her left arm. When she'd learned that all claiming ceremonies were witnessed, she'd gaped, then accepted the blindfold and Grigg's promise. *"Trust me, love, you won't be aware of anything but our hard cocks filling you up."*

When we reached the center of the room, Grigg released her and nodded for the ritual chant to begin. The words were from an ancient language on our world, the cadence odd to my ears. "Bless and protect," was chanted in the ancient tongue.

"Do you accept my claim, mate? Do you give yourself to me and my second freely, or do you wish to choose another primary male?" Grigg prowled around us like a barely leashed beast as I pulled Amanda's back to my chest, my hard cock resting against the crease of her plump, round ass.

Grigg's barely contained lust blasted both of us through our collars, amplifying my own need to be buried balls deep inside her. I groaned as the musky scent of her arousal rose like a cloud of the sweetest perfume.

"I accept you, I want no others." Her voice was breathy, her breasts rising and falling as she spoke.

"Then we claim you in the rite of naming and will kill any other warrior who dares to touch you."

Grigg made his vow and I made mine, bending down to whisper the words against the side of her neck. "I will kill to defend you or die to protect you, mate. You are mine, now, forever."

The chanting stopped temporarily as male voices spoke in unison, "May the gods witness and protect you."

Amanda shivered but stood bravely before us, waiting for us to claim her forever, her beautiful body on display making my hunger for her a rage in my blood.

I grinned at Grigg, eager to get on with it, but I waited for Grigg to make his move. His dominant nature was riding him hard and the more he dominated her, the more orgasms we could coax from her lush, responsive body. And Grigg was generous in his play, making sure we all lost our fucking minds.

"On your knees, Amanda. On your knees, and spread them wide."

———

GRIGG

MY MATE SETTLED on her knees before me without argument or hesitation and I felt her pleasure spike as I took control. She was so damn responsive, so sweetly giving that I had played out dozens of possible scenarios in my mind for this moment. Positions. Ways to make her come.

But seeing her on her knees before me, naked, blind and completely trusting unleashed something dark and needy within me in response.

"Open your mouth. I'm going to put my cock on your lip, and you're going to lick off all my pre-cum. It's going to heat your tongue, whet your appetite for our cocks. Do you understand?"

"Yes."

That one word caused my cock to jerk and I grabbed it by

the base, moving into position. Rav stood behind her waiting, and I realized I wouldn't have been able to share her with anyone else, with another warrior as dominant as I. Rav was mine and somehow that calmed the primitive animal within me when he touched her.

"Rav, lie down on your back and fuck her with your tongue."

My second was beneath her in seconds, his head sliding between her open thighs with ease. I watched with satisfaction as our mate's hips jerked at the first hard swipe of Rav's tongue as she sat upon him. She gasped and I knew from the connection of our collars that Rav's tongue had gone deep, fucking her as I'd ordered, making her wet and ready for my cock.

When she was moaning and fighting Rav's hard hold on her thighs, I finally settled the seeping head of my cock on her plump lips. "Suck me down, Amanda. Fuck me with your mouth."

I should have been prepared, but Amanda's hot mouth swallowed me down in one hard, fast glide, her tongue working my cock with a rough eagerness that nearly made me come too soon. Too fucking fast. My balls drew up and the need to come built at the base of my spine.

I wouldn't last and I hadn't even gotten insider her pussy yet.

Grabbing her hair, I gently pulled her head back until my cock popped free. I couldn't wait. I'd wanted to make this last, to make it go on forever, but now that we were here I just wanted her to be mine.

Now. Right fucking now. I wanted her collar blue, my seed in her womb, my second's cock in her virgin ass, bonding us together forever.

"Stop, Rav."

Amanda whimpered in protest but I simply lifted her from the floor, lifted her to my chest, positioned her wet pussy over my cock, and lowered her onto my aching shaft as she hooked her legs about my waist. The intensity of her reaction, of the feel of my cock filling her, spreading her open rocketed through her and straight to my collar, and my cock plumped in response. I was holding on by my fingernails.

The claiming chair was three steps away and I hurried to it, taking my place in the oddly angled chair. The seat was designed for fucking, leaning me and my mate back at just the right angle for Rav to stand and take her from behind.

I settled quickly, grabbed Amanda's thighs and pulled her forward onto me and my aching cock, spreading her ass cheeks wide for Rav's conquest.

Amanda whimpered, and the sound was music to my ears as she tried to shift in my grip, to rub her eager little clit against me and find relief. But she couldn't have it, not yet. Not without both of her mates inside her.

"Fuck her, Rav. Now."

AMANDA

I WAS SPRAWLED across Grigg's hard chest in some kind of reclined chair, his cock so deep and thick I felt like I was going to die if he didn't move. Grigg's hands grabbed my bottom, spreading me wide.

"Fuck her, Rav. Now."

"Yes! God, yes! Fucking hurry. Hurry. Hurry." I wiggled and shifted my hips, trying to press my clit to Grigg's rock-hard abs, but he denied me, holding me so tightly that I couldn't move at all, I could only feel.

And wait.

God, the wait was going to kill me.

"Hold still, Amanda." Grigg's voice was a deep throaty vibration that just made me hotter, more desperate. Squeezing my thighs, I lifted myself off his cock just enough to slam down again with a groan of satisfaction, ignoring my mate's command.

"Rav!"

Grigg's released my ass and I celebrated my victory, lifting myself and fucking him again until his hard palm came down on my sensitive bottom. *Smack!*

"What did I tell you, Amanda?"

What did he tell me? All I could think about was his cock. "I don't know."

"Your pleasure is mine. Your pussy is mine. Don't move your pussy, mate. I told you to hold still."

"No. No. No." I whimpered the words and Grigg's hand landed with a quick bite of pain on the other side.

The heat rolled through me and I stilled, not because I was avoiding another spanking, but because at long last, Rav touched me.

He spread the lube around my ass with first one finger, plunging deep as I whimpered and moaned, desperate for more, desperate for them to fill me up and fuck me. Their fingers, the plugs, had all worked and I was ready for Rav's cock.

Patiently Rav worked two fingers inside and what felt like a third. The stretching sensation was painful for a moment, the burning a familiar ache that added to the chaos of sensation stampeding through my body, through the collars, through Grigg's cock and Rav's thundering heartbeat. I felt it all. I needed it all.

"Please."

I nearly sobbed with relief when I felt the plump head of Rav's cock press forward slowly. Grigg's hands returned to my ass, pulling my cheeks apart, opening me up for Rav's possession. Knowing that my mates were going to take me, fuck me, fill me somehow made me hotter, wetter, closer to release.

God, how far down the dark path had I traveled?

The thought was fleeting as Rav pressed forward still, past the slight resistance of my inner muscle, then slowly worked his way into me, filling me completely.

I was stuffed, filled with two cocks, my ass burning from Grigg's spanking and my mind empty and waiting. I belonged to these men, my mates, and I would give them anything they wanted, anything they needed.

They were mine.

The connection, the bond through the collars was intense, our arousal and pleasure a bright and fierce circle, swirling up and up.

"Fuck her, Rav, slowly," Grigg growled.

Rav pulled halfway out of my ass, then slid back in. I whimpered, panting, so close to the edge. The feel of both of them, of two cocks, hot and thick, filling and claiming me was too much.

"I won't last long."

Rav's confession drove me higher, and my pussy clamped down on Grigg's cock, making him moan my name.

"Amanda. Gods, I love you."

Something wild and reckless rose within me at his desperate confession, something dark and needy and utterly fearless. I shoved against Grigg's chest, pushing myself up enough to reach back and grab Rav's hair. I pulled him forward with my right hand, his large body wrapped around my back, and kissed him with teeth and tongue and so much fucking need that I wanted to devour him, never let him go.

Beneath me, my left hand spanned Grigg's throat, squeezing him gently but hard enough to stake my claim.

Rav groaned into my mouth, his hips moving a bit harder, a bit faster in and out of my ass, pushing me onto Grigg, making me wild.

I shoved Rav away and turned to Grigg, kissing him with the same wild fever that owned me now. He buried his hands in my hair, his hips rising and falling like a piston, fucking my pussy as Rav claimed my ass.

I rode them like a wild woman, one thought more powerful than an ocean of words in my mind.

"Mine."

It became my litany, my chant, as I was fucked by both of them. Between them. I connected us together, made us whole. *Mine*. I didn't know if the thought was mine, or Grigg's or Rav's. It didn't matter when their hoarse cries of release filled the room, when their seed filled me up, when the burning heat of the seed marked me. I screamed my release, the bonding essence like a lightning bolt striking my clit, my ass, my pussy. I shattered, took a breath, lost myself again and again, each shift of their hips enough to push me over.

We slumped into each other, catching our breaths, but the men did not pull from me. They remained deep within, hard and thick. Soon enough, they grew harder still, their cocks growing, stretching me impossibly more and they fucked me again, slowly this time, their spent seed easing their way, their hands and mouths everywhere, their whispered words of love and adoration sinking into me until I surrendered completely, my orgasm this time a slow, spiraling explosion that left me too weak to hold up my head, my limbs shaky and unresponsive.

The collar burned as I lay on Grigg's chest, Rav covering us both, all of us out of breath and numb with pleasure.

Grigg's hand rose to stroke my chin, lifting my head out of the way to inspect my collar. Rav leaned around to take a look.

"What is it?" I asked, my voice scratchy from my cries of pleasure.

"You belong to us now," Rav answered. "Forever."

"Your collar is blue," Grigg added, so I would understand.

Their words brought tears to my eyes as emotions I'd been

holding back rushed to the surface. Relief. Pride. Joy. Belonging. Family. And love. The last emotion rolled through me and I was helpless before it, a feather swept along in the current. I was free now, free to give myself to them, to love them, forever.

I felt their love, their sated pleasure through the collar. It was open and just as free.

"I love you both, so much." I sobbed and they soothed me, sheltering me in their embrace, protecting me as the stress and chaos of the last few days finally took its toll. In their arms I was safe, and I let it all go.

I let myself love them and felt their love for me in return.

"Mine. You're both mine." The words were a jumbled mess, but my mates heard me and simply tightened their hold. We were one and nothing would ever change that.

———

Ready for more? Read Tamed by the Beast next!

When Tiffani is mated to an Atlan warrior believed lost to mating fever, she will stop at nothing to save him, including sneaking into an Atlan prison to seduce his beast....

Sick and tired of the dead-end path her life is taking, Tiffani Wilson heads to the nearest Interstellar Bride processing center to start over. She's promised an amazing mate, an Atlan Warlord who will not only relish her plus sized body, but heal her lonely heart.

Commander Deek of Atlan has lost control of his inner beast and sits in an Atlan prison cell awaiting execution. Unfortunately, nothing can save an unmated male.

When Tiffani's transport to Atlan is denied due to her mate's unstable condition, she will stop at nothing to save him and the life she was promised. Her mate is out there, he's in trouble, and she knows she's the only one in the universe who can save him.

Deek and his inner beast take one look at Tiffani's soft, lush body and know they will do anything to possess her, even if it means pushing her sensual limits or taking her over his knee. But it's not just Deek's tenuous hold on the beast that stands in the way of their happily-ever-after, for Deek's descent into mating fever was no accident, and his enemies will not surrender so easily.

Click here to read Tamed by the Beast now!

A SPECIAL THANK YOU TO MY READERS...

Want more? I've got *hidden* bonus content on my web site *exclusively* for those on my mailing list.

If you are already on my email list, you don't need to do a thing! Simply scroll to the bottom of my newsletter emails and click on the *super-secret* link.

Not a member? What are you waiting for? In addition to bonus content (great new stuff will be added regularly) you will always be in the loop - you'll never have to wonder when my newest release will hit the stores—AND you will get a free book as a special welcome gift.

Sign up now! http://freescifiromance.com

FIND YOUR INTERSTELLAR MATCH!

YOUR mate is out there. Take the test today and discover your perfect match. Are you ready for a sexy alien mate (or two)?

VOLUNTEER NOW!

interstellarbridesprogram.com

DO YOU LOVE AUDIOBOOKS?

Grace Goodwin's books are now available as audiobooks...
everywhere.

LET'S TALK!

Interested in joining my **Sci-Fi Squad**? Meet new like-minded sci-fi romance fanatics and chat with Grace! Be part of a private Facebook group that shares pictures and fun news! Join here:

https://www.facebook.com/groups/scifisquad/

Want to talk about Grace Goodwin books with others? Join the **SPOILER ROOM** and spoil away! Your GG BFFs are waiting! (And so is Grace) Join here:

https://www.facebook.com/groups/ggspoilerroom/

GET A FREE BOOK!

JOIN MY MAILING LIST TO BE THE FIRST TO KNOW OF NEW RELEASES, FREE BOOKS, SPECIAL PRICES AND OTHER AUTHOR GIVEAWAYS.

http://freescifiromance.com

ALSO BY GRACE GOODWIN

Interstellar Brides® Program Boxed Set - Books 6-8

Interstellar Brides® Program Boxed Set - Books 9-12

Interstellar Brides® Program Boxed Set - Books 13-16

Interstellar Brides® Program Boxed Set - Books 17-20

Bad Boys of Rogue 5

Interstellar Brides® Program: The Colony

Surrender to the Cyborgs

Mated to the Cyborgs

Cyborg Seduction

Her Cyborg Beast

Cyborg Fever

Rogue Cyborg

Cyborg's Secret Baby

Her Cyborg Warriors

Claimed by the Cyborgs

The Colony Boxed Set 1

The Colony Boxed Set 2

The Colony Boxed Set 3

Interstellar Brides® Program: The Virgins

The Alien's Mate

His Virgin Mate

Claiming His Virgin

His Virgin Bride

His Virgin Princess

The Virgins - Complete Boxed Set

Interstellar Brides® Program: Ascension Saga

Ascension Saga, book 1

Ascension Saga, book 2

Ascension Saga, book 3

Trinity: Ascension Saga - Volume 1

Ascension Saga, book 4

Ascension Saga, book 5

Ascension Saga, book 6

Faith: Ascension Saga - Volume 2

Ascension Saga, book 7

Ascension Saga, book 8

Ascension Saga, book 9

Destiny: Ascension Saga - Volume 3

Interstellar Brides® Program: The Beasts

Bachelor Beast

Maid for the Beast

Beauty and the Beast

The Beasts Boxed Set - Books 1-3

Big Bad Beast

Beast Charming

Bargain with a Beast

The Beasts Boxed Set - Books 4-6

Starfighter Training Academy

The First Starfighter

Starfighter Command

Elite Starfighter

Starfighter Training Academy Boxed Set

Other Books

Dragon Chains

Their Conquered Bride

Wild Wolf Claiming: A Howl's Romance

SUBSCRIBE TODAY!

Hi there! Grace Goodwin here. I am SO excited to invite you into my intense, crazy, sexy, romantic, imagination and the worlds born as a result. From Battlegroup Karter to The Colony and on behalf of the entire Coalition Fleet of Planets, I welcome you! Visit my Patreon page for additional bonus content, sneak peaks, and insider information on upcoming books as well as the opportunity to receive NEW RELEASE BOOKS before anyone else! See you there! ~ Grace

Grace's PATREON: https://www.patreon.com/grace goodwin

ABOUT GRACE

Grace Goodwin is a USA Today and international bestselling author of Sci-Fi and Paranormal romance with over a million books sold. Grace's titles are available worldwide on all retailers, in multiple languages, and in ebook, print, audio and other reading App formats.

Grace is a full-time writer whose earliest movie memories are of Luke Skywalker, Han Solo, and real, working light sabers. (Still waiting for Santa to come through on that one.) Now Grace writes sexy-as-hell sci-fi romance six days a week. In her spare time, she reads, watches campy sci-fi and enjoys spending time with family and friends. No matter where she is, there is always a part of her dreaming up new worlds and exciting characters for her next book.

Grace loves to chat with readers and can frequently be found lurking in her Facebook groups. Interested in joining her **Sci-Fi Squad**? Meet new like-minded sci-fi romance fanatics and chat with Grace! Join here: https://www.facebook.com/groups/scifisquad/

Want to talk about Grace Goodwin books with others? Join the **SPOILER ROOM** and spoil away! Your GG BFFs are waiting! (And so is Grace) Join here:

https://www.facebook.com/groups/ggspoilerroom/

Made in the USA
Middletown, DE
07 November 2024

63603787R00117